Tales from West Africa

OXFORD COLLECTIONS

Tales from
West Africa

Retold by Martin Bennett

Illustrated by Rosamund Fowler

UNIVERSITY PRESS

OXFORD

UNIVERSITY PRESS

Great Clarendon Street, Oxford OX2 6DP

Oxford University Press is a department of the University of Oxford.
It furthers the University's objective of excellence in research, scholarship,
and education by publishing worldwide in

Oxford   New York

Auckland   Cape Town   Dar es Salaam   Hong Kong   Karachi
Kuala Lumpur   Madrid   Melbourne   Mexico City   Nairobi
New Delhi   Shanghai   Taipei   Toronto

With offices in

Argentina   Austria   Brazil   Chile   Czech Republic   France   Greece
Guatemala   Hungary   Italy   Japan   Poland   Portugal   Singapore
South Korea   Switzerland   Thailand   Turkey   Ukraine   Vietnam

Oxford is a registered trade mark of Oxford University Press
in the UK and in certain other countries

British Library Cataloguing in Publication Data available

ISBN 978-0-19-275076-1

10

Printed in Great Britain

Paper used in the production of this book is a natural,
recyclable product made from wood grown in sustainable forests.
The manufacturing process conforms to the environmental
regulations of the country of origin.

For Emmanuel and Natasha

West Africa, it has been said, is a place where stories grow on trees. All over the region, folk myths and legends are still very much alive. The star character in a great many of the tales is the trickster, albeit he has several different guises and alibis. Part rogue, part pint-sized hero, he takes on the dubious laws of the jungle single-handed. What he lacks in sheer bulk or strength, he more than makes up for in natural cunning. Whether confronted by a roaring lion or a rustling famine, his 'trickishness' is a sort of passport to survival in a far-from-ideal world. True, he sometimes over-reaches himself and, much to everyone's amusement, is caught and punished. But it is never for so long that he cannot soon wriggle himself free to star in the next story, trickish and ingenious as ever . . .

One of the trickster's most famous incarnations is Kweku Ananse, the spider/man from Ghana, though there is also a trickster spider in neighbouring Togo and Ivory Coast and as far away as Hausaland in Northern Nigeria where he goes under the name of Gizo. We must also not forget Ananse's almost identical twin across the ocean in the West Indies. The second trickster to star in these tall tales retold is Tortie the Tortoise from Southern Nigeria and Cameroon. The third trickster, the hairier Hare, hails mostly from Senegambia where he lollops to the name of Leuk. Leuk is also rumoured, by the way, to be a distant cousin of that American upstart Brer Rabbit, so the mythical trickster has a way of slipping across boundaries of space as well as time . . .

In retelling these stories my thanks are due, among others, to Comfort Jackson (now my wife), Atemkeng Achanga, William Dodou, Isaac Mensah, and then to some students of Federal Government College, Kaduna who I recall improvising several legends into short, very amusing plays quick as you could utter the word 'Storiosity'. And if the versions in this small collection have changed in the telling, becoming a bit shorter here, a bit taller there, then let me end with the old saying, 'A tale that flies through many mouths has many feathers.'

Contents

Preface by Moonlight

First imagine some moonlight. There must always be moonlight, though it may be sunniest noon and you are in the classroom, the moonlight purely in your mind. Honey-coloured moonlight or silver or flashily platinum to see shadows by, the colour does not matter.

Now, in the moonlight, imagine a tree as large and gnarled and shady as widest wish can measure.

Underneath the tree, imagine a group of children—four years old or fourteen or four times fourteen, the age does not matter.

Now, in their midst, imagine a story-teller.

And if he (or she) starts multiplying into two or three or more people before your eyes, don't worry. It's part of the story-teller's spell and traditional storiosity. Or maybe he (or she) will multiply into not-even-people-at-all. So, in the world of myth and legend, skulls have been heard to speak, a mosquito has fallen in (and out of) love with an ear, a spider given political broadcasts, the trickish tortoise pleaded his case in court as skilfully as any lawyer. Or so one story goes . . .

Yes, the story-teller is an actor with a chest full of different voices. And a producer, script-writer, make-up artist, stuntman, and interpreter of languages, animal and human. In fact, he (or she) is nothing short of a sort of one-person cinema, a walking-talking variety show worth his weight in televisions and more.

The children, listening, watch his every change of face and gesture. And, watching, they listen to his every change of voice. Now he becomes a creeping tortoise, now a scuttling eight-legged spider, now a lolloping, leaping hare. Drum hanging from his shoulder, now he bangs a drowsy listener to attention, fires off an imaginary hunter's gun, aims a blow at the hero's enemy. Now he is a run-of-the-forest hunter, now a squeaking triple-headed ghostess. And somewhere between these shifts, he may also remember to be himself, but not for long . . .

But hush! I hear a hush of moonlight. Our story-teller pulls his robes about his shoulders, adjusts his drum. Somewhere at the back of his tongue the characters are composed and ready. Ah, moonlight! Ah, storiosity! Our first tall tale retold can hardly wait to begin . . .

Head Over Heart

OR, HOW MONKEY TRICKED SHARK AND SO SAVED HIS LIFE

O nce upon a story, a million moons ago, there was a monkey. Now, there can be no monkey without a tree. And so there was a tree. And the tree of this monkey happened to be by the sea—not for the sake of the rhyme only, but because that was where it was.

Now, this tree was full of mangoes and more mangoes, enough to feed a herd of elephants if there had been one nearby. Which there wasn't. The monkey never had to go to the farm or the market or the supermarket. Instead, he would play all day amidst the tree's branches. Then, when he got tired, he would sit down on his favourite branch to rest, and pick some mangoes, fresh as fresh could be. Sometimes he did this because he was hungry. Sometimes he did it for the not-very-particular reason that he liked throwing mangoes into the sea below and watching the splash they made. It was so pretty, the way the ripples spread out one after the other across the still, blue water, the sun flashing dancingly between.

A shark, who had made a habit of basking and swimming nearby, liked it too. Every time a fresh uneaten mango fell into the water, the shark would eat it. Mmmmmm! Mangoes made such a delicious diet after eating fish all the time, fish and more fish and the occasional jellyfish for dessert.

Every day Monkey would amuse himself by throwing mangoes into the sea and watching the ripples. It was just as entertaining as watching television. So, every day, the sea his playground, the shark would amuse himself by pointing his nose above the water and catching the mangoes between his teeth. He did not bother to spit out the stones. What is the stone of a mango to a shark who can swallow a man, bones and everything? Yes, even a monkey if necessary . . . But for now, at least, mangoes and more mangoes were enough. Monkey plucked and threw them. Shark caught and ate them. It was a nice arrangement. Despite belonging to different elements, soon Monkey and Shark had become friends.

Now, friends the world over respect the saying: 'One good turn deserves another.' Soon Shark decided, in his own sharkish way, that it was time to pay Monkey back for his kindness.

'Mister Monkey, your mangoes are so sweet,' barked Shark, opening his jaws above the water. 'Look, it's high tide I repaid you. Why not jump down from your tree and I can take you to my people. Then you will see what sharkish hospitality is really like.'

'But what about my fur?' replied Monkey. 'You know we monkeys do not like getting our fur wet. No, the sea is fine for throwing mangoes into and watching the splash they make, but as for swimming in, that is another thing completely.' Monkey looked into Shark's jaws, less happy about accepting his friend's offer than his friend was in giving it.

'No problem,' said Shark, surfacing above the water once more. 'You don't have to get wet at all. All you have to do is jump on to my back and hold on to my fin. I will swim close to the surface of the water, don't worry. I promise you a waterproof ride all the way. So you are coming, I hope. You know, I hate to take no as an answer.'

'Well, all right,' agreed Monkey, for want of a better reply.

Monkey jumped down from his tree. Soon he was on the sea-shore, hopping this way and that to avoid the oncoming waves. Shark steered his body closer and Monkey climbed drily on to his back.

'Ready? Hold on tight!' And with a flick of Shark's tail, off they went into the Bight of Benin, for that was what this part of the ocean was named. Shark swam; Monkey sat, holding on tightly to Shark's fin to balance better. The waves whizzed by and Monkey looked back to see his tree getting smaller and smaller till it was out of sight completely. Already they were in mid-ocean; water, water everywhere, tilting this way and that.

'Is it . . . er . . . is it far?' enquired Monkey weakly. He was beginning to suffer from worry and sea-sickness combined. Worse still, he remembered the old sailors' song: 'The Bight of Benin, O the Bight of Benin! Few come out though many go in!' and could not get it out of his head.

'No, not far at all,' Shark assured Monkey through his teeth. 'Only, Monkey, there is just one thing I should tell you. You know what a good friend you are to me, and I would not tell you otherwise. It's just that our chief—Chief Sarkin Shark III, Ruler of the Bight of Benin and Anti-Protector of the Guinea Coast—is dying from a strange illness. We have given him cod-liver oil, crushed sea-horses, squid's ink, boiled anemones but all to no effect. There is only one thing left that might cure him . . . '

'And what is that?' asked Monkey, gripping Shark's fin still tighter.

'A monkey's heart. Chief Sarkin must eat a monkey's heart. It's the only medicine. Now I'm sure you wouldn't mind providing us with your own?'

'I would be only too happy to help. Only . . . only, you see, Mister Shark, how can I donate my heart to your chief when I haven't brought it with me.'

'Haven't brought it with you? But how?' exclaimed Shark.

'So you have not heard that we monkeys leave our hearts hanging up where we sleep. It may sound a bit unscientific, but don't ask me why, except it's an ancient custom among us. You see, we only use our hearts at night. Now, if you had told me earlier about your chief's illness, I could have arranged to bring my heart with me. What a pity!'

Shark ground his teeth and groaned.

'It's true. I would even cross my heart if I had it with me! Of course, you can go ahead and kill me if you like,' offered Monkey. 'But imagine what will happen when your people open me up afterwards and find there is no heart inside me? What will the other sharks think of you then? I would hate to see you embarrassed before your chief, especially considering his critical condition. I am only telling you this as a special friend, you understand . . . '

6

'Oh, what shall I do? What shall I do?' wailed Shark. (Being one of them himself, he knew how merciless his tribe could be.)

'We will just have to swim back to land. There is nothing else for it,' concluded Monkey. 'Then I can go and fetch my heart down from where it is hanging. Don't worry, it won't take long.'

Following his passenger's advice, Shark did a U-turn there in mid-ocean. Countless waves later, there was Monkey's beloved mango tree rising above the sea-shore. The fruit dangled down in fat green clusters and the sun caught in the branches like many-coloured ribbon.

Shark swam closer to shore and when his stomach was flat against the sand, Monkey dismounted from his back.

'Don't worry, Mister Shark. I will go and come back just as soon as I can fetch my heart from its hanging-place,' assured Monkey. Then he scampered across the white sand to his home-sweet-home. Meanwhile, Shark was left to swim round and round in vicious circles, waiting for Monkey to bring his heart as promised. But Monkey's cheerful 'go-and-come-back' was definitely more a matter of 'go' than 'come-back'. If Shark had had legs, you can be sure he would have used them as quickly as you can snap your teeth. As it was, he had only a fin and a tail, as useless on dry land as Monkey's fur was useless in water.

One hour later Shark was still swimming around. His tail was aching, his stomach was growling, and his head was getting dizzier and dizzier. Worse still, if Monkey did not come soon, they would miss the outgoing tide. Shark thought of Chief Sarkin Shark III, Ruler of the Bight of Benin and Anti-Protector of the Guinea Coast, of whether he was dead yet or not, of what punishment he (Shark) might expect on his return.

'Look here, Monkey! How much longer are you going to keep me waiting? Don't you realize our chief may die at any moment? Can you find your heart or not?'

'So you think I am a fool!?!' Monkey's voice echoed down from the safety of his tree. (Recovered from his seasickness, he was merrily eating mangoes.) 'You think I've not seen through your sharkish tricks?!? No, Mister Shark. You can carry on swimming round till your tail drops off for all I care. I am not coming. Not for all the salt in the ocean. Just leave me to eat my mangoes. And as for my heart, it is in the right place. It's not hanging anywhere, but is here beneath my chest just as it should be. So you think I can give it away so easily? Never, not even to a girlfriend, let alone to a shark like you. No, I am not stupid. No monkey's heart for you. From now on, no mangoes, either.'

And so Shark, heartless creature that he was, had no choice but to swim back towards the centre of the ocean. What happened on his return—whether he was punished or not—has been washed away by the tides of time. Not that Monkey in his tree cared a groundnut one way or the other. Or a Mango. By the skin of Shark's teeth he had learned his lesson.

And that is why, kind listeners, you will never see a monkey bathing in the sea.

Nor, for that matter, will you find a shark eating mangoes.

The Glue of Greed

I t was getting to harvest time in the village. Ananse,
World Champion for Greed and Fast-eating
(Flyweight Division), could hardly wait. Yam! Yam!
Yam! Pounded yam as high and round as a hill! Ananse's
stomach beat like a drum at the thought of it. But . . . .
There was a problem.

Ananse wanted all that food for himself. And himself
alone. The idea that anyone should share it with him was
most distasteful. And when those to share in it were his
own family, his own flesh-and-stomach, that was more
distasteful still. Whatever the laws of heredity said
otherwise, he would not let it happen. No way! And as he
and his family made their way home from the farm,
Ananse thought out a plan. He was not Ananse for
nothing. He would show them that when it came to eating
he could beat anyone, even his own family, spidery
greedy-guts that they were.

Then that same evening at table a very strange thing
happened.

The first bowls of groundnut soup and pounded yam
had just been emptied.

9

'More!' cried Kwesi.

'More!' cried Kojo.

'More!' cried Kwame.

'More!' cried Kobbina, last but by no means least, completing the hungry chorus.

'Ha . . . ba! What terrible children!' scolded Mrs Ananse, otherwise known as Anansia. 'What terrible appetites! Like holes that get bigger and emptier with filling. Why, you would eat the table if I put sauce on it! Don't you know that the second helping is always reserved for your father? Wait till harvest comes, then you will be able to get your second helpings, and even third and fourth ones if you like . . . '

Mrs Ananse turned to her husband at the head of the table.

'Now, my dear, have some more groundnut soup, you know it's your favourite.'

But instead of automatically holding out his bowl as usual, Ananse just sat there and said, 'I'm sorry, my sweetie, but you see . . . I am not hungry . . . '

'Not hungry!?! Have my ears heard correct? How possible? Is this my very own Ananse talking or someone in disguise? Ananse refusing food? And after all the pounding I have done? Or perhaps you have been taking food outside? My husband, look me in the eyes and tell me.'

'No, it's not that, my dear, don't vex! It's just that since this afternoon on the farm, I have not been feeling quite myself . . . Er, if you will excuse me, I think I had better go to bed and rest.'

Mrs Ananse readily agreed. For the first time in history, ancient or modern, her husband refused to eat. It was a sign that Ananse must be very ill indeed.

10

'Ooooh! Aaaaah! Ooooooh!'

All night the small hut echoed with Ananse's cries of pain until the walls themselves seemed to ache in sympathy.

'Ooooh! Aaaaaah! Oooooh! Aaaaaah!' again and again until Mrs Ananse decided it was time to call up the traditional doctor on the bush telegraph system. A waiting and keen-eared monkey picked up the message and flew with it through the trees as fast as his long arms would carry him. A final leap and he reached the doctor's surgery. There was no time to lose. The doctor packed some leaves and potions into a bag and made his way through the shadows to Ananse's hut. By the time he arrived, Ananse was almost too weak to speak.

To his expert 'How are you?', Ananse could only groan from beneath the bedclothes, 'Worse . . . and . . . worse.' Each word, it seemed, threatened to be Ananse's last.

The doctor's visits increased. The bush telegraph had not been so busy in moons, and at all hours its branches could be heard crackling and rustling beneath the messenger-monkey's weight.

'I cannot understand it,' the traditional doctor said to Mrs Ananse in private. 'I have tried every leaf and root in the rain forest and not a few from the savannah as well. But your husband is not responding to any of them.'

'Oh, doctor!' poor Mrs Ananse replied, wringing her eight legs. 'Please do something. Anything. This afternoon I offered Ananse a groundnut, just a tiny groundnut. And Ananse told me it was too much, that if he ate it he might vomit. Oh! Oh! I am too old to become a widow!'

The following day it seemed her worst fears were about to come true.

Ananse raised a trembling leg from beneath the bedclothes on his bamboo bed and beckoned to his wife. 'Anansia . . . ' he gasped in an uphill voice. 'Bring me . . . a . . . pen . . . and paper. Yes, my dear . . . My time . . . has . . . has come . . . like it must come . . . to us all and . . . and I wish to make my last will . . . and . . . testament . . . My wife . . . I leave all . . . all my earthly possessions to you . . . and . . . the children . . . Only . . . My wife . . . Listen very carefull . . . y . . . When they bury me, bury my cooking things . . . with me . . . Don't forget to put plenty . . . plenty of salt and pepper . . . and dried shrimps . . . You know, my dear, how I like . . . dried shrimps in my soup . . . Yes, in the next world . . . my spirit will need feeding . . . Also, put plenty of kerosene . . . Who . . . who . . . who knows whether kerosene is scarce in the next world as . . . as it is on earth . . . Next . . . Listen well . . . Anansia . . . this is most important of all . . . Take my coffin to the middle of the farm . . . Bury me right in the middle . . . so . . . so . . . my spirit can be near . . . near . . . you and protect you . . . But . . . but . . . but . . . I am . . . too . . . tooo . . . weak . . . toooo . . . '

And with a last sigh Ananse said no more.

'Speak, Ananse! . . . Speak, my husband! . . . Speak!'

But it seemed that Ananse was dead.

The whole village mourned. Libations were poured; speeches and tributes were made in Ananse's honour, first by Tortoise, his international rival in trickery, then by the other animals. It was a sad occasion indeed. Even the laughing hyena was weeping. The elephant shed tears by the bucketful, and the dog howled and howled. There in the special circular-shaped coffin Ananse's body rested in state, his eight arms tucked neatly by his side, his mouth set in an unearthly smile. 'Perhaps he is dreaming about heavenly and never-ending mountains of fufu,' Mister Monkey thought to himself, only he was too polite to say it.

The same afternoon, amidst the beating of drums, the firing of muskets, and the piping of flutes, Ananse's coffin was loaded on the ox's back and carried to the middle of the farm exactly as Ananse had instructed. A hole was dug and the special circular-shaped coffin lowered into it with a rope. The last soil dropped on the coffin lid, and the mourners filed sadly homeward.

The sun went down on the empty field and slowly, silently, rose the moon.

Slowly, silently, in time with it, rose the lid of the coffin.

Then, out of the coffin, slowly, silently, appeared an arm, then another, then another, then another, all the way up to eight. Then, slowly, silently, rose the head of Ananse; not all, just the eyes rolling beadily around on stalks, taking in the lie of the land to make sure nobody was watching.

The field was empty.

There in moonlight and the shadows Ananse came out of his coffin and held his stomach with laughter.

'So, I tricked them this time!' he snorted through his furry nostrils. 'I really tricked them this time! They thought I was dying. But I wasn't dying at all. When I refused that groundnut, what they did not know was that I had my own secret supply under the bed all the time. Oh, the fools! But I am feeling hungry again. Let me not waste time . . . '

And there in the yam field, Ananse started pulling up his yams as fast as he could get his eight hands on them. Yams and more yams, the very ones he and his family had spent all those back-breaking months planting! Soon he had a pile of them, the fattest and the tastiest he could find. Then he brought out from his coffin his small kerosene stove and his kingsize pots and his cooking oil. He shaved and cut up the pile of yams, added the necessary ingredients, lit the stove, and hummed tunes as if to hurry the cooking along.

At last, Ananse's private feast was ready. Himself as host, chief honourable guest, and other invitees combined, soon he was eating, eating, eating to his heart and stomach's content. Several pots of food later, he had finished. Ananse lowered himself back into his coffin, skilfully scraped soil on top and in no time was sleeping off the after-effects of his massive meal.

An hour later along came the sun. And along came Ananse's family, their shadows spidering out in front of them. The field was just as they had left it.

Or almost.

Things are not always what they seem on the surface. Imagine their surprise when they dug a foot-or-two below the soil and found half of their harvest missing. Had they got the wrong field? But no. One memory might be wrong, but not five memories together and all in exactly the same way. What thief, then, could have done it? Not to mention the insult to their late and dear departed. If the thief had no sympathy for the dead, he might at least respect them and leave them to their eternal rest.

What was to be done? 'Gong! Gong! Gong!' It was not long before the village crier had been informed and he was summoning the elders and local wisemen for a meeting. What was the best method to catch this yam-stealer and disturber of the dead as well as of the living? With calabashes of freshly-tapped palm wine on hand to provide refreshment and inspiration, the elders scratched their heads through more and more speeches and the orang-utan scratched his armpits. Several thousand words and many proverbs later they had come up with a definite plan. They could not catch the thief in any obvious way; he was obviously far too clever for that. No, they would catch him with a trick even the trickiest trickster would not be able to wriggle free from. They would . . . Well, we will come to that later . . .

Meanwhile, back in the yam field, night after night, when his family and everyone else had gone home, Ananse rose from the coffin, pulled up some yams, cooked them on his secret stove, then ate them . . . and ate them . . . and ate them . . . and was still eating them when, one night, in mid-mouthful, he stopped. Before him in the moonlight stood a skinny, scruffy-looking figure stretching out his arms.

'Hey, you! So you don't know who owns this farm? Go away, you rogue, you hear!' shouted Ananse as bravely as he could manage.

But the figure did nothing. Just stood and stood and stood there like a towering dummy.

'U-Uh! So you don't know Ananse, Kweku Ananse, World Champion for Greed and Fast-eating?! Or perhaps you are deaf? Whoever-you-are, I said get out from this my farm or I will make trouble, I am telling you!'

Still the weird figure just stood there. And stood there. And stood there.

This was too much for Ananse.

'So you are dumb as well as deaf, are you? We will see about that! If you won't respect the living, at least you might learn some respect for the dead. So you don't know

15

I have just risen from the grave? You don't know that I am a ghost? And you know what ghosts can do, don't you? Or do you want me to give you a demonstration of my supernatural powers? I am warning you. Uh? . . . Uh? All right, Mister Man or Whatever-You-Are, enough is enough . . . All right, if, er, words won't frighten you, take this!'

And there in the moonlight, Ananse gave the figure a definitely unsupernatural slap as mighty as the mighty Igor himself. First—Thwack!—with one arm and then . . . and then . . . But Ananse's arm had stuck.

'Ho! So you think you can lay hold of me like that, do you? And on my own farm too? All right, then, if I can't slap sense into you, let me kick sense into you! Take this!'

His leg stuck.

'Huh! This is getting serious. Take this then!'

His next leg stuck also. Hmmm. This was more than serious. Ananse, who had in his time beaten the hippopotamus and the elephant in a single duel, had never met such an opponent before. He wiggled. He squiggled. He jiggled. He wriggled. And he would have even ziggled if such a word existed. In this world or the next, what kind of opposition was this?

Ananse had just five blows left. For blow number four he unleashed a kick straight out of a Kung-Fu film with the same sticky result. Then he let fly a not-so-flying drop-kick. It flew through the air and also struck with no more effect than a sausage-fly against a window-pane. Three blows left: a karate chop, a left-hooked punch, a final slap, then an even more final desperate and almighty headbutt. Ananse was now stuck—from his furry head to his eight hands-or-feet. Worst of all, his opponent had not yet uttered a word.

16

Ananse's pride and anger now turned to beggarly fear.

'Look, Mister Man-Or-Whoever-Or-Whatever-You-Are, I beg. I am sorry for what I said just now, about you being a thief and me being a ghost. I didn't mean it . . . Just let me go. If you are hungry, I will share my food with you if you like . . . Or if the food is not enough, I can always cook some more . . . All right, how many yams do you want? Fifty, a hundred? Just let me go. All right, take the whole harvest, I don't mind. Only put me down. I am aching. Oh, Mister Man, please, pleassse!'

Little did Ananse know that he was not speaking to a man at all. Not even a deaf-and-dumb one. No, the man was . . . a scarecrow, covered with the stickiest, gummiest gum from the stickiest, gummiest gumtree the forest could provide. However much Ananse begged or shouted, it did not listen but just kept on holding Ananse till along came the sun, big and red, at the far end of the field.

And along with it came Ananse's family.

If Ananse's death had been a shock, if the disappearance of their yam harvest had been another, then here was the shockingest shock of all. There was their dear and late departed risen from the dead and dangling in mid-air. If Ananse were really a returning ancestor or spirit, certainly no ancestor had returned to earth in such a form. Or so soon. Was it really possible to reach heaven so quickly? Or the other place?

Ah, the disgrace of it!

Before anyone dared to bring Ananse down from his peculiar sticking-place, he was forced, painfully, shamefully, to confess everything, from his eating half the yam harvest right down to his refusing that single groundnut because he had a whole store of them under his bed all the time. No wonder the traditional doctor had rustled and shuffled his leaves in vain.

Poor Ananse! How small he felt! Somebody brought a pot of boiling water and, limb by limb, he was unstuck and brought back down to earth. As punishment, all Ananse's cooking implements were confiscated indefinitely. Until the next yam harvest, Anansia refused to cook anything for him but bread and water. And, of course, she did not forget this time to check under Ananse's bed for any hidden supplies of groundnuts.

'All right, if you refuse to cook for me,' Ananse threatened, 'I will go and marry a second wife who will, just you wait and see!' But then Ananse had become so infamous, no female would have him, not even Mrs Mantis who had eaten up twenty husbands already and was hungrily awaiting another one. What was left but for Ananse to go back home for his evening bread and water?

And that is why, kind listeners, when you see a spider hiding there so tinily in the corner of your house, it is only Ananse. Still, after all these years, he has not forgotten his lesson.

A Debt Made Profit

OR, WHY MONKEYS LIVE IN TREES

Are you in debt by any chance? Is Austerity biting you too hard, turning your plus into minus, robbing your tea of sugar, filling your pockets with holes, making a vacuum of your fridge? Have you got angry creditors queuing and stamping outside your door, pestering your life? If not, so much the better. If yes, then this story is here to help you. Presuming you are a tortoise, that is . . .

Tortoise picked up his carved walking stick, put on his embroidered cap, and announced to his wife, 'I am going out for a while, my sweet! Some business matter in town. I won't be long.'

What Tortoise did not announce was that he had just spied his friend Monkey bounding full-speed towards the house. And what again Tortoise did not announce was that Tortoise owed him three month's salary. After all, in these days of inflation what wife wants to hear such things?

So Tortoise crept out through the back door. A few steps later he was hidden in the tall grass to listen to what went on while he was 'away'.

A minute later there was Mister Monkey, a very angry Mister Monkey, hammering at Tortoise's door.

'Tortoise, open up. Open up at once, you hear! I have had enough of your dirty tricks. Open up, I say!'

When the door did open, there was no Tortoise inside the house. Only Tortesca, Tortoise's long-suffering wife. Awkwardly Monkey began to eat his words. And they tasted very prickly and embarrassing indeed!

'Oh, er, madam, I am dreadfully sorry. I mean, I didn't realize it was you. It's just that poverty can make you very bad-tempered. But about your husband, would he be at home by any chance? I have one small matter to discuss with him.'

'My husband? What a pity! He left just a moment ago.'

Monkey fought down his anger.

'Of course, Mister Monkey, if you would like to leave a message, I would be very happy to pass it on when he returns.'

'No, madam. Just tell him I will be back, that's all. Yes. I'll be back. He will know what for.'

Turning on his tail, Monkey left as penniless and hungry as he had come. Not only hungry, but also angry. The two feelings mingled inside him and, as if electrified, twitched his long arms this way and that. 'That Tortoise! If I could get hold of him, I would break his head like a coconut. Yes, I would . . . I would . . . ' But Monkey's anger at this point got the better of his words and he went on his way, cursing Tortoise under his breath.

Tortoise quietly watched his debt-collector vanish

round the bend, then crept out of his hiding place. A few slow steps and he was back at his own front-door.

'Any visitors while I was away, my sweet?' he enquired in his most innocent voice.

'Only Mister Monkey,' came Tortesca's reply from the kitchen.

'Oh, yes, it must have been about that expensive contract he promised to award me,' Tortoise lied, making up the contract on the spur of the moment. 'But you know these contractors, how unreliable and trickish they are. Still, we should hope for the best. But, now, Tortesca, what about my dinner?'

'It's nearly ready. Just let me finish grinding these groundnuts and the soup will be on the fire in no time . . . '

Tomorrow came.

And with it along came Monkey. Tortoise still owed him all that money, yet as things stood, Monkey could not afford a single groundnut. Yes, a hungry man is an angry man. And a hungry monkey is an angry monkey. Especially if he is hungry through no fault of his own, but just because one trickish Tortoise refuses to pay his debt.

'Hmmm, Tortoise will see pepper today. Just let him wait and see!' Monkey mumbled to himself as again he knocked—Rata-Ta-Tat!—on Tortoise's door.

But again it was the same story as yesterday. No Tortoise. No money. Only Madam Tortesca. And then, even more infuriating, the delicious smell of groundnut soup wafting from the kitchen at the back. He sniffed and his appetite made him feel dizzy. Yet even monkeys have their pride. No, he would not beg. What else could Monkey do then but leave, his debt still unpaid?

'Come back tomorrow, if you like,' Tortesca called out to Monkey's shadow.

Another tomorrow came. And again came Monkey, hungrier and angrier than ever. And each time there was Tortoise hiding in the long grass at the back of the house till Monkey had gone.

'Hmmm, this is getting too much,' complained Tortoise into his groundnut soup. 'So a tortoise can no longer be at peace in his own home, or what? So he thinks he can disturb our privacy just anyhow? No, Tortesca, this busybody of a monkey needs to be taught a lesson, no matter what his business might be.'

And in his trickish mind Tortoise weighed one trick against another, which trick might work, which trick might not.

'Let me see now . . . Uh-huh . . . Uh-huh . . . No, not that . . . Let me see,' the words echoed from some studious corner inside Tortoise's shell. 'Uh-huh . . . Yes . . . That's it . . . That's what I will do . . . ' And Tortoise stuck out his head, a triumphant smile crinkled across his mouth.

It was time to call Tortesca, his better half and partner in trickery.

'Tortesca, my sweet, come! Er, now, my dear, there's one small thing I want you to do for me.'

'Yes, Tortie, what is it?'

'This Monkey is getting too troublesome for his own good. The way he is always disturbing you in your housework and your cooking, I don't like it at all. Now, I have just been thinking what to do about it. Next time Monkey comes clattering and battering at our door, this is what I want you to do. I want you to turn me upside-down, you understand?'

'Upside-down?' laughed Tortesca.

'Yes, upside-down. Don't laugh, I am serious. Then, after you have turned me upside-down, place me in the kitchen in the same place that you usually keep your grinding stone, I think you get me? Then, when Monkey comes and asks where I am, tell him I am out as usual. Then . . . then . . . But I will explain the rest later.'

However peculiar or tortuous it was, Tortesca agreed to do what Tortoise had asked.

Next day, at the crack of dawn, there was Monkey clattering and battering at Tortoise's door and shouting.

'All right, Tortesca,' whispered Tortoise into the pinhole of her ear. 'You know what to do. Now do it.'

Tortesca lifted her husband into mid-air . . . One . . . Two . . . Three . . . And there Tortoise found himself upside-down and right in the place where Tortesca usually kept her grinding stone. With his head and feet tucked inside his shell and with his shiny flat stomach, you could hardly tell the difference.

Bang! Bang! Bang!

Again came Monkey's knocks, like a machine gun. You could hear the anger inside them. This time Monkey meant business. It was get back his money or die, that was what it was!

But Tortoise meant business also.

Tortesca opened the door.

'Where is Tortoise?' Monkey demanded without stopping for so much as a greeting, his hair sticking out at the most unusual angles.

'Good morning,' greeted Tortesca nevertheless, bravely and politely standing her ground.

'No, it is not good morning, Mrs Tortoise. It is bad morning. Now I don't want any nonsense this time. I said, where is he?'

'Mister Monkey, I am terribly sorry, but he has gone out again. I can't help it, really I can't, that my husband is such a walk-about . . .'

'I have had enough. And more than enough. I mean, how? How!?!?! Every time the same story: playing me up and down like a small boy, like I am the one who owes him, not the other way round. Well, I won't stand for it! I won't stand for it!'

And as if to emphasize his point, Monkey started to jump up-and-down and from side-to-side, waving his long arms about like a windmill in a hurricane. If he had been a bomb, he would have exploded on the spot. Instead, he continued his furious dancing and prancing and started to look for something to throw. It didn't matter what. (Head tucked inside his shell, Tortoise 'The Grinding Stone' was having great difficulty stopping himself from laughing aloud: Mister Monkey was acting exactly according to plan.) Barging his way past Tortesca, first Monkey threw a tumbler out of the window. Then he threw a cooking pot. Then he threw some tomatoes. Then he threw a bar of soap. Then he threw a plate. Then he threw a flying saucer, and then . . . And then he threw the grinding stone.

Or what he thought was a grinding stone.

Powered by all the might of Monkey's anger. Tortoise flew through the air like a rocket, scattering leaves and nesting birds along the way. His head tucked safely inside his shell, he prepared himself for quite a long journey. But even the most powerful rocket has to land sometime. The green flashed past him and the occasional blue blur of sky. A hanging bat stood on its feet in amazement and the parrot repeated a prayer. Tortoise buried his head still deeper inside his shell and waited for the coming crash.

Ten, nine, eight, seven, six . . . he counted the seconds off before splash-down, and regretted he did not have a parachute.

Meanwhile, back inside the house Tortesca was weeping.

'So is this how you behave, Mister Monkey?' she sobbed into her apron. 'And to think that was my prize grinding stone, the very grinding stone my Tortie gave me as a wedding present. How am I going to get another one? How am I going to grind groundnuts and vegetables for my husband's favourite soups? Oh, Monkey, so you want to disgrace me before my husband and before everybody else? It is too bad of you!'

Monkey, who had been so angry before, was now highly (or lowly) embarrassed. His anger had blown itself out like a tornado and now he felt only regret. After all, it was not Tortesca who owed him money. And, who knew, perhaps Tortoise owed his wife as well. Knowing Tortoise as he knew Tortoise, it was quite likely. Monkey should be feeling sorry for Tortesca, not angry at her. He bowed his head and scratched behind his ears in shame.

'Madam . . . Madam Tortesca, I am so sorry. I didn't mean to offend you. I just lost my temper and . . . '

And as Monkey was groping for excuses and eating his words, if nothing else, there was a sound at the door. Tortoise was back from his brief journey in space.

'Ah, Mister Monkey, so here you are at long last. I am so glad to see you. Welcome. Indeed, welcome. I have been expecting you all these days now so I can pay off my debt. I think my wife told you. But let me just go and greet her. Then she can prepare us some nice soup to eat. You look like you could do with a decent meal. After all, you have lent me money, and one good turn deserves another . . . '

Tortoise went into the kitchen. Then he saw his wife in tears. What had happened? What terrible thing had Monkey been doing during his absence? Tortoise turned to Monkey and demanded an answer with immediate effect.

'Oh, Tortoise, forgive me, I beg. I threw your wife's grinding stone into the forest.'

'Threw her grinding stone into the forest, what on earth do you mean?' Tortoise's head recoiled back inside its shell in false surprise.

'Yes, that is why she is so upset.' Monkey hopped from one leg to another in further embarrassment. 'You see, I didn't mean to throw away your grinding stone. Only I was angry because you had not paid me my money and . . .'

'But, Monkey, how unfortunate! Very unfortunate indeed! Why, I can hardly believe it! You see, that grinding stone was the very place where I kept your money. You know how armed robberies are common these days. Well, I wanted a safe place nobody would think of looking in. And what better place than the hole inside a grinding stone! In fact, I had almost come to see that grinding stone as my private bank. And now you tell me you have thrown it, account and all, into the forest. How very unfortunate for both of us!'

Monkey groaned and moaned and started jumping up-and-down again.

If he wanted his money back, what choice had he but to enter the forest and look for it? Back into the trees Monkey scampered, moneyless as he had come, to start his search.

Of course, he never found his money. Or Tortesca's grinding stone, even though it had been standing before his two eyes and talking to him only moments before.

Tortoise never paid his debt, either.

Sometimes he hears Monkey swinging and crashing through the trees outside his window. (Or—this story is so old—perhaps it is one of Monkey's great-great-grandsons.) Sometimes, also, it crosses Tortoise's mind to tell Monkey (or Monkey's great-great-grandson) what really happened that day and save him all that wasted energy and bother. But swinging and crashing through the trees has become such a habit with Monkey that he would probably never listen. Not to Tortoise. Nor to you. Nor to me. Next time you go to the zoo or are walking in the forest, and you see a monkey, try telling him this story and see. You can bet your last groundnut that soon he will turn on his tail and carry on looking, looking, even though he has forgotten what for.

A Bite Too Far

OR, THE CROCODILE REVENGED

There are daggers in men's smiles, goes a saying.
How much more then in the wicked grin of a
crocodile?

Those saw-like teeth, that leathery old nose to sniff
the next kill, those sinister yellowish bulbs of its eyes
grazing the surface of the river, that reinforced and
bone-cracking tail: all are warning enough. Or at least
to any but the foolish and easily edible. I mean, would
you like to share a room or flat with a crocodile? No
fear, not for all the salt in Timbuctoo. A sly old tyrant,
the crocodile rules the river and make no bones about
it. Hmmmm, Crocodile! A thoroughly unpleasant
character if ever there was, a bully with a mouth big
enough to swallow a goat at one bite (if any are
foolish enough to go that close). Even a man when
necessary. Or woman. Or child. To tough-skinned
Crocodile it makes not a shred of difference. Snap-
snap-snap-snap, just like that, as simple and clear-cut
as a rag to a well-oiled pair of scissors. And without

his shedding as much as a tear. No, not even a crocodile one.

If Crocodile were a human being, he might be sentenced to life imprisonment, put on a perpetual diet of bread and water, or something like that. But, needless to say, the crocodile is not a human being, but a crocodile. Crocodilus carnivorus, for the scientifically-minded. How to get rid of one is not so easy. Use a rifle, you might say. Remember, though, that this tall tale retold is an ancestral one. When it was first told many many great-great-great-grandfathers ago (and great-great-great-grandmothers), rifles were not yet invented. Nor muskets. Nor blunderbusses. Use a spear then. Or a bow and very big arrow. Hmmm? A spear or arrow against a crocodile? You might as well try sticking a drawing pin into an iron bar. How *do* you get rid of a crocodile then, presuming you have one in your river and he is making a daily meal of your inhabitants and not a few between-meals snacks as well?

The answer, or one answer anyway, is the subject of this tale. If you have a river nearby and the crocodiles in it happen to be peace-loving, polite, and even fearful, or they have migrated to other waters, this might be the reason why . . .

Once upon a sun and moon, many suns and moons ago, there was a village; there was a village, and there was an old, old crocodile.

And most important to our tale, there was a drought, so bad even the fish were thirsty. Just like the Electricity Corporation tend to take off light just when you most need it, so the heat of the drought had taken off water. The frogs had stopped croaking long ago, even though it was supposed to be the mating season. The gods of rains were rumoured to have deserted their cave and left for the rainforest, a few hundred miles south. Ponds and lakes had turned into areas of muddy scales, their edges turning upward in the sun. If and when a cloud appeared, the villagers would come out to greet it as if it were a visiting Head of State. But the cloud would never pay attention, just continue sailing wispily to wherever clouds sail. The wells in the land had also dried up. Where there had been twinkling water, now there were shafts of twinkling dust and perhaps the skeleton of a careless goat or antelope at the bottom like a discarded basket.

Mother Earth drew in the air between her cracked lips.

'It is so hot you could fry an egg on a grinding stone,' she sighed. 'And not a drink of water in miles. Now, my daughter, take this calabash and go to the river and fill it with water. I know it's far, but there's no other choice. And make sure you don't spill any on the way back. Water is worth its weight in blood these days, let alone in gold.'

'Of course, mother,' the daughter agreed, her tongue feeling like leather in her mouth. She picked up the giant calabash, adjusted her head and body gracefully to the shape, and set off for the river, the speed of her feet accelerated by the scorching ground below. The mother waited. And waited. Still after a couple of hours the daughter had not returned. The sun had travelled nearly three-quarters of its way across the sky. Whilst some daylight still remained, Mother Earth decided it was time to send her son to find out what had happened.

'It's not like your sister to stay long like that. Go, my son, and see if your sister needs help. Perhaps with her slender body and neck, the water was too heavy for her.'

The son ran off towards the river, his shadow following behind him and not a cloud up above to get in its way.

Again the mother waited.

Again nobody returned. Dusk fell, deep blue then purple, and brought with it comparative coolness. But still no rain. No daughter. And now no son, either. Mother Earth knew her son was not the careless walk-about type to get himself lost anyhow. What had happened?

Only Crocodile's greedy stomach knows . . .

The days burned by. The wells got dustier and dustier. The sun got fiercer and fiercer, like a hungry lion. More and more people went to the river to collect water. More and more people disappeared. One person went missing trying to fetch water; another person went missing trying to find him.

To the human beings in the village the drought might be a matter for anxiety and mourning. (The marks for missing persons on the trunk of the silk-cotton tree in the village square had almost reached the first branches.) To cruel Crocodile the drought was more a matter of *'Bon Appetit!'* as the French say before sitting down to dinner. One man's loss be the crocodile's gain, Crocodile reasoned ruthlessly to himself. Man, woman, child, or beast: whatever and whoever came down to the river's edge, there was Crocodile waiting for it. Or him. Or her. A whack of that massive reinforced tail, a snap of those enormous jaws, a sawing of those teeth, and . . . and . . . It is too dreadful to think about . . .

And when it was all over, Crocodile would go slinkingly off and sleep away his meal under his favourite tree, just like nothing had happened.

The villagers had an unhappy choice before them.

Either they stay put in the village and perish slowly from thirst, or they venture down to the river and perish quickly between Crocodile's teeth. If you can call that a choice. Catastrophe or disaster, they could take their pick.

To say the situation was serious was even a joke when set against what was actually happening. Something had to be done before more people died and those marks for missing persons on the village's silk-cotton tree started climbing into the highest branches. One day the Village Chief decided to call a meeting.

'Bong! Bong! Bong!' The village gong resounded across plain and now dried-up forest, a sort of bush telephone before telephones had been invented. By evening, elders from miles around had gathered beneath the silk-cotton tree. They looked sadly at the marks scarring the trunk and shook their heads. Another bong of the gong, and the meeting began. And if the traditional welcome of palm wine had been left out, it could not be helped. All the palm trees had dried up long ago.

'Gentlemen,' began the Chief, waving his cowtail switch ceremonially this way and that. 'A toad does not jump in the daytime for nothing. Now, we all know how serious the situation is; I have summoned you here to hear your suggestions. Now, no condition is permanent, not even the life of a crocodile. What we must decide is how to get rid of this monster in our midst, this man-and-woman-and-child eater, this greedy-machine, this tyrant who wears his teeth like a crown. But let me sit down and leave the floor open for your ideas.'

An elder got up to reply: 'Thank you, Chief, for your fine words. Things are serious, very serious. But we must take hope. Crocodile might have teeth and jaws to be proud of. What he lacks, gentlemen, is brains. Or any brains capable of thinking further than his stomach. No King as God, we have a proverb. How much less right then has a brainless crocodile to rule over us? Now, to every problem there is a solution. My solution is emptying the river of water. This calamity of a crocodile has been thirsting us to death. You do me, I do you. Let us now thirst him to death likewise and likewiser!'

But likewiser or not, there remained the question of how? How, indeed? A river cannot be changed just like that. Just as soon try moving mountains or the sea. The strongest witchdoctor would not dream such a feat possible. There must be a better solution.

'I, for my part, have another solution,' declared a second elder. 'If we cannot empty the river, I suggest we fill it in.'

Again there remained the question of how? A river was stronger than anything human arms could throw at or into it, especially when the arms were weak from thirst.

'No, no, no. These solutions won't do at all,' began a third elder. 'I who have studied African Electronics and Thermodynamics suggest something more scientific. Let us heat the river to boiling point, centigrade or fahrenheit, it doesn't matter which. That way the crocodile will die and be punished for his crimes at the same time. The river which is now his unholy paradise will thus become his purgatory. This my method will also give us the extra pleasure of being able to eat him as he has been eating us. Hmmm, boiled crocodile pepper soup, what a dish that will be! Also the river will be free again for us to drink to our thirst's content.'

The suggestion was an appetizing one indeed. But again there remained the question of how? How to heat water in pots, that was easy. But to heat water in a river?

Again the elders racked their brains in vain. The third elder's scientific theory seemed to have got the better of his practice.

'Gentlemen,' countered another elder. 'I am sorry to say it, but these your solutions, however scientific, will not hold water. No, I have a better solution by far. You can bet your lives on it. Now listen. To get rid of this crocodile we simply need a goat . . . '

'A goat?!?' someone objected. 'But hasn't Crocodile had enough of our goats already?'

'Let me explain. As I was saying, we simply need a goat; a goat and a lot of stones, the sharper and the flintier the better . . . '

What seemed simple to the speaker still did not seem so simple to the audience, however.

'A goat? Some stones? What do you mean? Are you playing with our intelligence or what?' someone else objected.

'Not at all. Just listen and you will understand,' continued the elder, stroking his beard as though in time with the revelations inside his head. 'I have not got these my grey hairs for nothing. Here is what I mean. First, we will kill the goat. Second, we will take out the intestines, leaving only the skin. Then, where the juicy intestines were, we will put stones instead, the sharper and the flintier the better. Now, you all know what a greedy-guts and stomach-strong fellow Crocodile is. Do you think in his greed he will notice anything? Of course he won't. We will carry the specially stuffed goat to the riverside and leave it there. Crocodile will come out for his evening stroll and perhaps a bite to eat. He will see the dead goat. As sure as the law of cause and effect, his appetite will be aroused. He will approach the goat with the stones stuffed inside it, the harder and flintier the better. He will open that horrible big mouth of his. He will . . . '

But the smiles and cheers of the audience supplied the rest. Doubt turned to hopeful certainty.

Their plan was set.

All that remained was the execution.

A goat was found, killed, and stuffed just as the elder had craftily suggested. Soon, two of them carrying it on their shoulders, the villagers were marching to the river. To either side stretched the dusty remains of what had, in better and wetter days, been fields. The dust rose, the sun beat down, a few last stubborn leaves flashing back its light. Then the land dipped. The river was near, or the trickle it had been reduced to. The villagers spread out, hiding themselves behind the yellow reeds and watching for what was to happen next.

The goat-carriers looked this way and that as if they were crossing a motorway at rush hour. Then, when they were sure the river was clear, they ran forward and unloaded the goat on to the river bank, within range of Crocodile's eyesight. There was a long noon-baked silence. Nothing moved but a few flies. Had they got the wrong place? Some of the villagers were beginning to wonder. But then they saw him. Crocodile was taking his siesta amidst a pile of bones, his stomach sagging into the mud. He shifted his reinforced tail and yawned, so the villagers could see some threads of meat caught between his teeth.

'Perhaps he's dreaming of his next kill,' whispered one villager to another behind the cover of the reeds.

'Sssssssh! Look, he's waking up!'

Lazily keeping time with the heat, Crocodile opened one yellowish eye, then the other, and let the afternoon reveal what it had to offer. He sniffed through his snout, he cranked his head this way and that. Then he saw the goat. His pupils narrowed like the sights of a shotgun. What a gift! A kill, and he had not had to lift a claw for it. Just as if the carcass had dropped from heaven. And so fat as well. With an armoured sweep of his tail, Crocodile advanced, scattering bones behind him . . .

He adjusted the mighty hinge of his jaws and the razor-edged cavity of his mouth opened. No matter of manners or what others might say, he would eat that goat in one bite. Creaking a little from over-use, his jaws made an angle of eighty degrees in the sunlight, hung there taking aim, then came down upon their prey . . .

A horrendous sound rent the air, something between a crash and a squelch: the dental disaster of all time, stone against teeth, and stone winning teeth down. Molars, canines, incisors bit the dust. Like sickly lightbulbs, Crocodile's eyeballs nearly exploded from their sockets. On the riverbank the villagers leapt from where they were hiding and let out a cry of revenge and liberation. Yes, those who live by the teeth shall perish by the teeth. Not to mention what happened to Crocodile's stomach. No Andrew's liver salts, no aspirin, no herbal mixture could cure that stomach-ache! Crocodile was not able to eat or sleep for weeks.

Since that afternoon, you can be sure the crocodile in that river has kept his distance. As have his children. And grandchildren. No more meat for him again, animal or human. Toothless, or almost so, and his stomach disastrously digesting stones, the hardest and flintiest the villagers could find, Crocodile made his resolution: from now on he would only eat leafy vegetables, egusi, okro, and other softish foods. Then, when these were out of season, he would change his diet to beans and garri.

Yes, Crocodile had learned his lesson.

And the villagers had cured their water shortage. And got rid of their crocodile for good.

Wind and Stick Land Leuk the Hare Some Blows

Whoooeeeuuuwww! Wind whistled in his den, shuffled his invisible feet, combed his invisible beard, blew the sleep through his invisible nose, brushed his invisible teeth, downed an invisible cup of breakfast oxygen, then decided to take a ride in his invisible airbus (Zephyr 504 GL) which happened to be parked in the next cave. There was a whirr. There was a whoosh. The jet engine burst into life. Soon Wind was winding and wending and weaving top-speed ahead through the rainforest. Leaves rustled, water crinkled, hairs bristled, tendrils tickled, burrs twirled, dust dangled dizzily in mid-air. Mynah Bird felt her nest wobble beneath her. The baboon stroked his chin in wonder, and Owl's head rotated three hundred and sixty degrees. That Zephyr 504 GL with air-conditioning could move all right. Yes, Wind was on his way. Behind him the whole forest danced and swayed in a giant green samba right up to Leuk the Hare's garden and, there in the middle of it, his prize avocado-pear tree!

Ah, pears! They dangled down in dozens, dark green and delicious pendulums. A couple of weeks and they would be ready for harvesting. Their insides sweet and soft and golden on the tongue, their shape so smooth and round like . . . like . . . Leuk's mouth watered at the thought of them. And if he could not eat them immediately, he could always eat them later on. In fact Leuk had his crop numbered: four hundred pears for himself, two hundred for his greedy-guts of a family, twenty for special guests too important to refuse . . .

Imagine, then, Leuk's annoyance when Wind breezed through his garden at two hundred kilometres per hour, shaking his prize tree to the roots, knocking down pears as if they weren't even there. One minute Leuk's crop hung peacefully ripening in the sun, the next it was lying bruised and scattered over the ground for the commonest bushrat to carry off at leisure. And all without so much as a warning honk of the horn. So Wind had so little regard for Leuk or his stomach? The cheek of it! Or so Leuk, Dis-Honorary Professor of Gluttony, Forest University, was now explaining to his wife Lucia.

'My dear, things cannot go on like this. Ten times now Wind has come speeding through our garden in his airbus, knocking down pears like he owns the place, throwing his breath around. Vandalism and highly dangerous driving, that is what it is! And to think I put up a notice against trespassing. It is too bad, my dear. No, I am not going to stand for it. In fact, if I could lay my paws on the fellow, puffed up piece of nothing that he is, I would . . . would . . . ' But Leuk was so annoyed that words failed him and he nearly leapt right out of his chair.

'Lay hold of Wind? What are you saying?' Lucia

brought her husband down to earth. 'So you don't know that Wind is wind . . .'

'All right, all right. But whatever the case, Wind will compensate me. He will compensate me, you hear!'

'It would be difficult not to, my dear,' replied Lucia, lowering her ears which were naturally highly sensitive.

'I mean, why should common bushrats and ants and cockroaches enjoy while we go hungry? My stomach aches at the thought of it. Yes, even if I have to leap all the way to Wind's house . . .'

'Hear, hear,' urged Lucia, as one hare to another. 'Why don't you go then?'

'Why don't I go? Yes, I will go, hah, I will go right now!'

And with hardly time for a farewell kiss on the whiskers, off he leapt.

Across sunlit clearings, across moonlit clearings, across swamps, across thickets, Leuk travelled until days later he reached the forest's furthest edge. Beyond that stretched the land of Nowhere; somewhere beyond that the cave which was Wind's house. Now lurking in ditches, now lolloping with his ears back for extra speed, onwards and onwards Leuk travelled, spurring himself with the thought of those pears, and muttering, 'Wind will compensate me, yes, whatever the suffering, Wind will compensate me.'

At last, forelegs and hindlegs aching with the distance, Leuk arrived. Through a curtain of cobwebs and creepers came two sounds in one. 'Whoooeeuw-Grrrgh! Whooeuw-Grrrgh!' Wind was asleep, snoring mightily. To the strangely-shaped radar scanners that were Leuk's ears, it sounded like several jumbo jets starting up their engines at the same time.

'Wind, wake up!' Leuk shouted into the shadows. 'It's me, Leuk the Hare, the frisky one, the fast mover. Although I can't see you, I know you are there.'

Those regular 'whooeuws' and 'grrrghs' seemed to get tangled, changed rhythm, stopped.

'Now listen, Wind. What you've been doing just isn't fair,' said Leuk, adjusting his ears to a lower frequency. 'Don't you know my family is starving because of your careless driving? We pedestrians have to live as well. But every day you drive your airbus anyhow and knock down my pears before any of us can get our front teeth into them. I demand compensation with immediate effect.'

Knowing what a twister Leuk could be, Wind let the echoes of his protest subside, then replied, 'All right, Leuk, you whhhhill get your compensation; don't whhhhorry. Now you know I like travelling. North Pole, South Pole, Honolulu, Hawaaiiee, Turkey. There is hardly a country I have not visited . . . ' Wind paused to catch his breath. 'Now whhhen I wwwwas in Turkey I picked up a carpet . . . '

'A carpet, so what? What sort of compensation is that?'

'Wait and let me finissssh. This carpet is not just any run-of-the-house carpet. This carpet is a magical one.'

By the way he squeezed his face. Leuk was still not satisfied.

'Yesss, a magical one. Whhhenever you whhhhant anything, you just hhhave to say: "Carpet, spread!" and all your whhhishesss will come true, simple as that. Now whhhhill that do as compensation?'

'Well, if you say so, Wind. I just hope your words are not hot air, that's all.'

Wind brought out the carpet from a corner of the cave,

blew the dust off it, and handed it over to Leuk. The rólled-up carpet balanced on his head, Leuk was soon making his way back home, shuffling wishes inside his brain to make the time pass quicker. But was Wind's fantastic claim true or not? Leuk paused in his tracks and decided he had better hold a small experiment. Besides, he was getting hungry. He peered this way and that to ensure nobody was looking. He pricked up his ears and tuned them to a higher frequency. Then, loud and clear, he addressed the carpet.

'Carpet, spread!'

There was a distant tinkle of kitchenware; there was a scent of spices; there was a movement between the leaves as of invisible waiters. Against all the laws of nature and gastronomy the carpet had obeyed Leuk's wishful command. Spread out before him was the most delicious meal Leuk or anyone else could have desired: fufu, a minor mountain of it capped with shrimps, sweetcorn, and garden-eggs, all this islanded by a minor ocean of the richest palmnut soup. This was the main course. For dessert there was a specially-imported treacle-pudding and cream caramel, this followed by several calabashes of freshly tapped palm wine to wash the meal down. So a carpet could do all this? It might be incredible, but it was true and Leuk was certainly not going to ask any awkward questions. Instead he got up on his hind legs to make a special thankyou speech in Carpet's honour. And if Carpet did not also get up to reply, then carpets have their limits, even magical ones.

Leuk ate and ate and ate till 'his belly done full' twice over. Then with all that food swimming contentedly around inside him, Leuk rolled up the carpet, patted it affectionately, balanced it back on his head once more and sped back to meet his family. Lucia was at the door of their hut waiting, her paws against her waist.

'But what took you so long, my husband? I thought you had gone away completely!'

'Don't worry about that, my dear. But look. I have a surprise for you. Not just any prize, but a magical one!'

'A magical surprise?' enquired Lucia, looking at the rolled-up carpet.

'Yes. Here.' And after unbalancing it down from his head, Leuk rolled out the carpet so Lucia could inspect it. 'Just say the magic word, my dear, and any food you like is yours for the asking. The world is your oyster.'

But Lucia was not quite ready. Her wide face shrivelled into a frown.

'My husband, that is all very well and marvellous. But I hope you don't expect me to eat on that carpet until you have washed it. Look how dirty it is! You want me to get jaundice?'

Not wanting an argument, Leuk agreed. Off Lucia went to the village stream to wash the carpet. Then, when the carpet was washed and dried just like any other carpet, the whole family sat down to enjoy their promised meal.

'Now, Lucia, my dear,' Leuk proudly opened the proceedings, 'what special dish would you like to order? Any food you want you can have. The wind's the limit.'

'Mmmmm . . . Mmmmm . . . I think I will start with a local dish, groundnut soup with rice balls . . . Then I will go on to something foreign . . . Lobster à la Duchesse like they eat it in Paris. Then . . . Then I'll finish off with icecream and chocolate sauce, just like you told me you had on your visit to Brer Rabbit, your distant cousin in Florida.'

'No problem, madam, your wish is my command,'

decreed Leuk gallantly. Then he uttered the magic words: 'Carpet, spread!' just as Wind had instructed.

Five minutes passed. Ten, twenty minutes passed. Lucia was beginning to lose patience as was her growling stomach.

'Now, my dear,' Leuk encouraged. 'You know such luxurious food takes time to prepare. You should not expect immediate service. Probably the flight from Paris has been held up. Just wait a little longer . . . '

Leuk's plea fell on deaf ears. The magic was not working; the only thing that was spreading was Lucia's scowl. Leuk patted the carpet, although not as affectionately as before. He kicked it. He stamped on it. He ran circles round it. He kneeled in the middle and prayed on it. He kneeled at the edge and prayed to it. 'Daerps, teprac!' he said the magic words backwards. Then he translated them into Turkish, then into Hindi, then into Gujurati, then into Swahili, then into Arabic and a dozen other oriental languages. Still the magic was not working. Lucia's frown had now been round her face several times. But what could Leuk do? His family's complaints echoing all-too-familiarly in his head, Leuk was off once more to Wind's house.

A forest and a desert later he had arrived and was shouting, 'Wind, you wicked old walk-about! So you think you can trick Hare, King of the Tricksters, do you? Never! Ne-ver! Ne-ver-ver-ver!' The words echoed emphatically back from wall to wall of Wind's cave. 'That magic carpet you gave me stopped working after only one meal!'

'Hold your hair on, Big Ears,' Wind replied breezily, annoying Leuk still more and bristling the hairs along his back.

'Well, what are you going to do about it? I demand my compensation, com-pen-sa-tion-tion-tion!' The word echoed back.

'Don't you whhhhorry. You whhhhill get your compensation, quite all right. But I do hhhhhope you did not whhhhash the carpet. You realize—or perhhhhaps you don't—whhhhhashing is the one thing to destroy a magic carpet's magical powhhhhhers . . .'

Leuk groaned. So that was why.

'Now then, take this pot instead,' continued Wind sympathetically. 'Whhhhenever you whhhhant something, just say "Pot, pour!", simple as that, and you whhhhill get whhhhatever you whhhhanted.'

Again Leuk returned home, balancing the magic pot on top of his head between his ears. But, as with the carpet, he did not forget to test the magic before he arrived, especially after what had happened last time. 'Pot, pour!' he gave the magic word. The pot poured just as Wind had promised, no translation needed. 'Ah, suffer to gain,' proclaimed Leuk to himself half-way through his second feast. Yes, the pot had performed like a dream come true. It remained only to convince the doubting Lucia. Leuk continued on his journey and there she was, annoyed and anxious, waiting, by the door.

'So what is the story this time, my husband?'

Again Leuk explained.

Again Lucia disagreed. 'Magic pot or not, you can't expect me to eat out of it when there is all that grease and dirt inside? Let me wash it first.'

'Anything you say, my dear,' replied Leuk. Some minutes later, after the pot had been washed, all the family sat down to enjoy the meal they had been denied the first time. If it were possible they were even hungrier than before, hairy greedyguts that they were. The pears had by now run out completely and still the harvest was not ready. Again Lucia made her order, adding a prawn cocktail just for good measure. Again her husband commanded 'Pot, pour!' Again . . .

Well you can guess the rest.

Jumping up-and-down with disappointment, Leuk was back on the track to Wind's house.

'You puffed up old fool!' bellowed Leuk. 'You inflated piece of nothing! So you think you can throw your breath around like that. No, for a third and final time, no, no, no, no.'

Wind, who happened to be eating a hydrogen sandwich, listened to the all-too-familiar voice, the string of negatives echoing off his cave walls. 'Hmmmm,' he thought to himself. 'This is getting too much. So Leuk thinks I can be insulted by a hare. And in my own cave. No, not by a super-hare. It is high time our weird-eared friend learned his true size and position in the order of things. This time I will get rid of him and his greedy trouble-making for good.'

Wind turned to Leuk and breathed, 'Calm down, my small fellow. You are still worried about compensation, are you? Very whhhhell. Let me fetch this stick for you. Just say "Stick, thrash, hit, beat," and I promise it will not be like the other times. This time you whhhhhhill get whhhhat you asked for quite all right, just whhhhhait and see!'

'Okay,' Leuk grumbled into his small beard. 'I only hope this time your words prove correct or there will be trouble, I am warning you.'

And carrying the stick, he went on his way, Wind whistling him farewell. It was not long before Leuk was hungry.

46

In the kitchen of his mind Leuk composed the longest most exotic menu imaginable—from fresh bamboo shoots to wind-dried duck, groundnut soup to palaver sauce, corn-on-the-cob to cornflakes with strawberries, beancakes to chocolate gateau. Hungrily his stomach relayed a direct message to his brain. 'Stick, thrash, hit, beat!' commanded Leuk like a little field major. As if suddenly possessed of a life of its own, the stick stood to attention, then wrenched itself from Leuk's grasp. To the hare's amazement there came no promised food, no delicious palaver sauce or chocolate gateau, but blows, now to the blind spot between the hare's eyes, now to his legs, now to his stomach, blows and more blows, one after the other just like in a Kung-fu film.

'Haaaa! Huh! Haaaaah!' The stick seemed a Kung-fu master in disguise. No, this was no ordinary stick, but a magical one indeed, with several years' secret training in Japan. Needless to say, Leuk had forgotten all about his menu. Willingly he would have swapped a bowl of fufu for a suit of armour. All that mattered now was saving his own skin. 'Haaaa! Huh! Haaaaaah!' The stick hopped this way and that on its single leg, aiming blows with supernatural accuracy, Leuk's radar ears unable to do anything about them. 'Huh! Haaah!' Stick completed his barrage with a blow to Leuk's upper lip and that mark poor Leuk and hares everywhere carry with them even to this day.

'Haaah! Huh!' Stick chasing him, Leuk was soon running for the nearest river bank. After all, he who runs away, lives to fight another day. Yet however much Leuk leapt, crept, lurked, skulked, turned, twisted, put back his ears for extra speed, somehow Stick kept up with him. Leuk had no choice but to bury himself in the smallest cranny he could find. There on the one side was the unlucky Leuk. There, just a foot away on the other side, was Stick doing a hopping war dance and waiting for Leuk to come out . . .

At least until, some hours later, Wind drove past in his airbus, Zephyr 504 GL with built-in air-conditioning.

'All right, Leuk,' Wind called from the window. 'That is enough for now. I think you have learned your lesson.'

'Yes!' gasped Leuk, nursing that split in his upper lip. 'I will never be greedy again . . .'

Or not for a while . . .

Ananse Meets His Measure

OR, A LESSON IN AUSTERITY

Austerity this, austerity that, everywhere and everything Austerity. Austerity yams. Austerity rice. Austerity garri. Austerity soup (without meat). Austerity tea (without milk or sugar). Austerity ballpoint pens (without properly flowing ink). Even Austerity water at ten kobo a cup. The items mount up (or down) like a sort of reverse shopping list. Turning plus into minus, Austerity rules! Now it is filling your pockets with holes, now your meat pies with tasteless air. Now like some wrongway electrician it is replacing your lightbulbs with candles, now candles with darkness. Let us thank heaven that the sun and air are free and not subject to inflation!

Meanwhile, it is financial war. No more automatic plenty. It's time to fasten our money belts for the long hard journey down the straight and narrow. But enough of official broadcasts. What has all this talk of austerity got to do with ancestral folk tales?

Well, our tall tale retold tells how one day Austerity

caught up with Ananse the Spider and measured him in a way he never would have expected. Austerity measured him so well, in fact, he has never been the same since, no, not in a thousand harvests.

But we are jumping ahead of things.

At the start of our tale Ananse was round, round as a rice ball. Not even the most expensively-tailored robes could hide the roundness of that stomach. Ananse's shape was the wonder of all the local villages. It was as if Ananse was pregnant from eating too much food. Had it not been for his small moustache and beard, you might have mistaken Ananse for Mrs Ananse, Anansia by name, and the valiant long-suffering mother of Ananse's four children.

When, then, the day of the festival came round you can well imagine Ananse's excitement. Mmmmmm, all that lovely food and feasting! In his sky-blue specially-tailored robes and prestige six-storeyed and geometrically-coloured cap for very important occasions, Ananse sat outside his hut and smacked his lips . . . Then stopped . . . There was a hitch: Ananse had been invited not to one feast, but to four. Well, any normal person would choose one feast to go to, and decline the other three. However, for Ananse, expert in the arithmetic of trickery, such a solution was too simple. Too simple by three. Besides, Ananse was not a person but a spider. Yes, Ananse was Ananse, King of Greed. He was not content to attend one feast alone. He wanted to attend all four of them.

Mmmm . . . To attend all four feasts at the same time? Without cutting himself in quarters, how was it possible?

Ananse rubbed his stomach as if to find an answer.

Yes, that was what he would do . . .

'Kwesi! Kobbina! Kojo! Kwame! Come here, quick!' shouted Ananse through his nose.

Knowing their punishment would be a dinnertime without food if they disobeyed, Ananse's sons rushed to his call as fast as their thirty-two legs would carry them.

'Now, my sons, listen carefully,' Ananse said, pulling his sky-blue expensively-tailored robes about his shoulders. 'You know today is the day of the festival. Well, famous and very important personalities like myself have heavy responsibilities. It so happens I've been invited as special and honourable guest of honour four times over. I would hate to disappoint any of my hosts or dishonour their invitations. No, my sons, duty is duty, however difficult. Then I know how they appreciate my after-dinner stories. I have just been scratching my stomach and thought of a way of attending all four functions on the same day so none of my hosts will be offended. Now, this is what you'll do . . . '

The four sons listened closely, wondering what their father would come up with this time.

'My sons, I want each of you to find a long, long rope . . . long enough to stretch to the homes of my hosts. When you have the ropes, I want to connect them about my waist. Then each of you, carry your end of the rope to the home of one of my hosts . . . You Kwesi to host A, you Kwame to host B, you Kojo to host C, you Kobbina to host D.' Ananse had scratched a map in the dust to make his directions clearer. 'Now, when the food at each ceremony is ready, pull on your end of the rope. I will be in the middle . . . here . . . ' Ananse pointed at the place on the map. 'By the direction of the pull I will then know which of the four houses to go to and at what time. The ropes about my stomach will relay your information in a second. And I will be able to honour all four of my appointments. And eat four feasts instead of one!'

Ananse's sons marvelled at their father's cleverness. With his trick Ananse had succeeded in inventing his own personal telephone system before telephones had been invented.

Soon Ananse's sons were busy putting their father's plan into practice, scouring the forest high and wide for those special ropes. Eventually they were found, cut to the necessary length, then tied loosely about their father's stomach. Then, each carrying his own end of rope, the four sons set out down the different paths to the different feasts. Ananse stood in the middle waiting that call. Which rope would be pulled first and to announce which feast? Would it signal pepper soup or groundnut, palmnut soup or okro? It was a mouth-watering question.

Ten minutes, half-an-hour, one hour passed. Ananse's stomach growled impatiently and his prestige six-storeyed and geometrically-coloured cap for very important occasions began to feel distinctly out of place. 'Hmmm, these my sons, have they forgotten me, or what? Or perhaps they have decided to eat my feasts in my place? So, must I wait all day . . . ?'

Just then he felt a sudden tightening about his stomach. It was the call he had been expecting. His stomach transmitted its message to his brain, his brain transmitted its message back down to his stomach, his stomach transmitted his message down to his feet and one, two, three, four, five, six, seven, eight . . . There was Ananse speeding towards his first feast as fast as his legs . . . fast as . . . as . . . as . . .

But Ananse had stopped in mid-pathway . . .

About his stomach he now felt the second rope of the

second son announcing the beginning of the second feast tightening also. The first feast was ready and so, now, was the second . . . And it was no use protesting that the line was already engaged . . . Pulled in opposite directions, Ananse could go in neither of them. He was thinking, 'How terrible! What shall I do?' when he felt a third pull, then a fourth.

All four feasts had begun. And there was Ananse being pulled in all four directions at once like a wrecked compass. Poor Ananse! His private telephone system was working in a way he had never bargained for. Nor, for that matter, had Thomas Edison.

Ananse was being pulled so tight he could not even shout 'Help!' Here was an emergency call four times in reverse. He looked down to see his stomach getting thinner and thinner as the ropes did their work, wringing him, wringing him like a washerwoman will wring a piece of washing down at the village stream. Ananse's six-storeyed and geometrically-coloured hat for very important occasions tumbled to the ground; his eyes nearly popped out of his head; his legs spun like the rotors of a helicopter moving nowhere.

'Hu . . . Hu . . . Hu . . . ' Before he could utter a syllable or step a step more, Ananse had lost consciousness, those telephonic ropes twisted and tangled in as many knots as you can name.

An uncertain number of days and nights later Ananse woke up. There was a powerful smell of leaves, and moonlight was pouring in through an open window. Ananse was neither in heaven, nor in hell. He was lying on a bamboo bed in the traditional doctor's hut at the jungliest edge of the village. His sky-blue robes and six-storeyed geometrically-coloured hat hanging from the door, he felt the cool night breeze bathe his half-naked body. Then, in searing contrast, he felt a sudden pain about his middle. Ananse looked down to see what was happening. And his eyes rolled three hundred and sixty degrees in amazement: he himself might still be here on earth, but where on earth or beyond was his famous stomach?

Ananse could hardly recognize himself. What had been round was now concave. What had been fat as a riceball was thinner than a chewing stick.

Despite the pain, plus the uneasy feeling that at any moment he would snap in two, Ananse looked under the bamboo bed, he looked in the corners of the room, he looked under the bedsheets, he looked outside the open window and into the branches of the tree outside. Whatever it might say in the biology books, his fat rotund stomach had vanished. There was nothing else for it. He would have to call the doctor.

Ananse opened his lungs and shouted. But what came out was more like a whisper than a full-throated shout. Again Ananse shouted. Or tried to. Then he fell back on to the bed with the effort. The moments passed in moonlit silence. How could he be in such pain yet the night so peaceful, he wondered?

Then into the room shuffled an old man smelling of herbs and vegetables. It was the doctor. Ananse pulled the bedsheet about his half-naked body and demanded between gasps, 'What kind of medicine is this? Where have you hidden my stomach? So you don't realize its value or what? Give it back, you hear, or I shall show you pepper!'

As soothingly as he could manage, the doctor explained about how he and Ananse's four sons had found Ananse spread-eagled on the pathway, about the four ropes, and about the four tiring hours they had spent untying them from Ananse's waist. Why, the last knot had been so tight they had had to recite a special charm to loosen it. Then he explained how, after giving him artificial respiration, they had carried Ananse, still unconscious, back to the hut for treatment. In fact, Ananse's case was the strangest the doctor had ever had to deal with. If he hadn't seen it with his own eyes he would not have thought it possible. He had used all his powers and potions in finding a cure. Hardly a leaf in the forest had been left unturned. Ground this, boiled that— he had tried everything from a dried chameleon's tail to baobab juice, from leopards' spots to mango leaves. No, Ananse should not be angry; he should be grateful. In fact, he was lucky to be in the Land of the Living.

Ananse, the impatient patient, listened to the doctor's words and groaned in understanding. Needless to say, Ananse never got his stomach back. Instead there is only a waist thinner than the ballpoint pen (without properly flowing ink) with which I am writing this story. Yes, Ananse's private telephone system had done its work. Through wanting too much too soon, Ananse had lost everything, even his stomach. Where before he might have eaten four feasts in a row, had our story been different, now there is hardly room for a chocolate ant.

At last Austerity had caught up with Ananse and got his measure!

The Opposite Party

You may envy the spider the slimness of his waist. Although he will never tell you, Ananse's anatomy was not always like that. Once upon a time Ananse the Spider was round, round as a bowl of fufu. The way his waist got so slim was neither enviable nor admirable. One explanation we have heard already in 'Ananse Meets His Measure, Or, a Lesson in Austerity'. My grandfather (from whom I first heard the story) swears by his grandfather that his story is true. But there is another version of how Ananse's waist got so slim. For fairness's sake, here it is. I will leave you to decide which of the two tales retold is the taller.

Ananse with the stomach round as a bowl of fufu lived in a village, and like most villagers he was a farmer by profession. At least, when he was not being a trickster, his favourite part-time job. Now, farming does get boring sometimes, especially if you have just returned from a 'Round the World Tour' like Ananse had.

Ananse decided to liven things up by calling a party. Not just any party but a special two-in-one party. One: The party would be a celebration for 'Arrival' Ananse's safe return from his 'Round the World Tour'. Two: It would be his birthday party. Not that Ananse, born without a birth certificate, had any idea when his birthday was. He only knew that with a birthday party came birthday presents, preferably food. But Ananse was not just greedy. Nor greedier. He was the greediest. If his guests brought food, Ananse began to think to himself, how could he prevent them sharing in the eating of it? Ananse wanted to have all that birthday food for himself . . . alone. And eat it, too. But how?

Ananse's stomach, round as a bowl of fufu, began to relay messages to his brain and his brain relayed messages to his stomach and slowly Ananse worked out a plan. Yes, he would first select his guests, then he would . . . He would . . . But like all good plans he would keep the rest locked inside his head and tell nobody . . .

The first guest on Ananse's list was Farmer. Of course, Ananse did not forget to mention his birthday and somehow twist the conversation round to the subject of presents.

'Don't you worry at all, at all!' said Farmer looking up from his yams. 'It is harvest soon and yams are not my problem. I will bring you more than even you can eat. I'd be delighted, in fact . . . Only . . . er . . . Ananse . . . Don't invite Snake, I beg . . .'

'Don't invite Snake?' replied Ananse. 'But you know how he likes dancing and twisting to my highlife records . . .'

'Yes, but if you invite him, there would only be a quarrel. The two of us are sworn enemies, you see, and I would not want to break up your party . . .'

But glimpsing the look on Ananse's face, Farmer felt he had best explain some more. 'You see, Ananse, it is a long story . . .'

Now if there was one thing in this world Ananse could not resist apart from food, it was a story of any length or shape or tallness. No matter that once he had tricked Nyankopon, the Sky God, into handing over his store of stories. (But that is another story again for another place and time.) Ananse's storiosity was still not satisfied! At Farmer's mention of the 'Story', Ananse almost forgot his plan completely.

'Carry on, Farmer,' he said, all eyes and ears, storious as storious could be.

'Well, it was like this,' started Farmer, putting down his hoe. 'Once upon a sun and moon, many suns and moons ago, human beings like me could live forever. There was no death in those days, no wrinkles or crinkles or shrivelled old age. Human beings had a special relationship with Nyankopon, you see. Whenever somebody felt age overtaking beauty, he (or she) could send a message to the Sky God and the Sky God would promise to send a new skin fresh and wrinkleless as the morning he (or she) was born. All the men were delighted with this arrangement, the women even more delighted. No need for any expensive cocoa butter or skin-creams. No need for body-oil or lotions. Well, one day, at the request of his wife and his mother-in-law, one man decided to send off for a special supply of those fresh and wrinkleless skins. Nyankopon received the message by airmail. No problem at all. Quick as a flash he had the skins packed in a basket and ready for Kraman the Dog (and Dogsbody) to deliver. So Kraman set off with his cargo. However, the journey between heaven and earth being a long one, Kraman decided to take a rest along the way. He unloaded the basket of skins from his back and lay beneath the shadow of a cloud. Soon he was deep asleep when who should wriggle by but Snake—'

'You mean the same Snake I was planning to invite to my party?' interrupted Ananse.

'The very one,' established Farmer. 'Well, Snake saw Kraman the Dog lying there fast asleep and then he saw and opened the basket. All those beautiful fresh skins! Wriggling and wrinkled creature that he was, they were just what he needed. And so Snake stole the skins and slinked off into the bush. He has been using them ever since. Whenever one snakeskin gets wrinkled, he just sheds and puts on another one. I have asked him to give me the skins back a hundred times. Stick is my witness. But every time Snake refuses. "Farmer, go away! I found the sssskinssss and I am going to keep them," Snake hisses. "Anyway, how do I know they were meant for you. Have you got a reccceipt or invoiccce to prove it?" '

'But couldn't you have gone back to Nyankopon and told him about it? Surely he could have done something to help you?' asked Ananse storiously as ever.

'Well, that's another problem again. You see, Ananse, ever since that greedy Madam Armstrong hit Nyankopon with her pestle, Nyankopon has been nowhere to be found. He is far over the horizon and out of human reach. Not that Snake cares. You see these my wrinkled hands, Ananse? You see these creases around my eyes and mouth? It is that Snake who caused them. If it had not been for him, I could be young forever. And so could all other human beings. So now do you see why there would only be a quarrel if you invited him to your party?'

'Very clearly,' answered Ananse. 'Nyankopon forbid that I do such a thing! You yourself know by the skin of your face what a snake Snake is!'

'So you promise not to invite him?' asked Farmer.

'Never,' announced Ananse.

And he scuttled off as happy as could be. Not only had he added one more story to his store; his plan was working out just as he had planned it. And where did Ananse scuttle? Where else but to the very hole where Snake lay sleeping.

'Sssssss! Sssssssss!' hissed Ananse in Snakish. 'Sssssnake, wake up! There'ssssss going to be a party. There will be lotsssss of highlife recordsssss. I know how with your sssssslim and sssssslinking shape you like danccccing. I hope you will not refusssse the invitation. And, er, perhapsssss you can bring sssssome thing along to oil the proceedingsssssss. It'sssss my birthday, you sssssee, and er . . . '

'Sssssay no more, Anansssse! I'd be only too pleassssed. Only who elsssss is coming? Not Farmer by any chancccce?'

'Oh yessss,' assured Ananse between his teeth. 'By all means Farmer is coming. I jussssst invited him.'

'Excccellent. We have sssssome busssssinessss to dissscussss,' continued Snake, feeling the poison rise inside him and relishing a quarrel as much as Farmer had wanted to avoid one. 'Only do not invite Sssstick, pleasssse. That would really sssssspoil thingsss . . . '

'Of coursssse, I won't invite him,' stressed Ananse.

'Good. I'll get one of my new sssspotted skinssss out ssspecially then. Or should I wear a sssstriped skin insssstead. I assssume the party is formal dressss?'

'Any one,' finalized Ananse.

'Sssssee you there then,' said Snake. 'Only I hope you'll ssstick to your word, Ananse. About not inviting Sssstick, I mean?'

But already Ananse had his next guest lined up. Almost as soon as Snake's long back was turned, Ananse had done exactly what he had promised not to do, adding in his most wooden voice, 'And Stick, I hope you won't forget the present.'

'No way! If Stick can't keep to his promises, I don't know who can!' cracked Stick. 'Only don't invite Fire, whatever you do. It's just something in our make-up, but we can't seem to hit it off together. Then he is such a hot-tempered fellow, always flaring up over the smallest things. No, don't invite him. Unless, that is, you want your arrival and birthday party to be my farebadly and funeral ceremony as well?'

'But I would not dream of inviting Fire, Mister Stick.'

And so saying, Ananse continued on his trickish way. The bush path twisted and bent and twisted. There was silence and then a birdcall and then more silence. Then, filling the silence, there was a strange spitting, crackling, roaring sound. Round Ananse rounded another corner, then saw where the sound came from. Fire was dry-cleaning the bushrats and insects from his flaming red beard.

'Fire! Hey, Fire!' shouted Ananse, shielding his face and precious stomach from the heat. 'There is a party at my house and you are invited. I hope to blazes that you will come. You know there is never a dull moment when you're around!'

'Okay!' Fire roared back after a fit of coughing on his own smoke. 'But I am telling you, don't invite Water or your party will go out like that. I hope you get me?'

But already Ananse was redirecting himself to the nearest river to extend his next invitation.

'What a wonderful idea! Yes, I'd be delighted to come,' gushed Water, his eagerness dampened only by his warning, 'Only, Ananse, make sure you don't ask Sun.

The two of us are best kept skies apart or you'll find I have suddenly evaporated from your presence. You see, we have never really got along since I and my very extended family visited him one Sunday and flooded out his house and compound. From the smallest raindrop to the widest ocean we were all there. But instead of receiving us properly, Sun and his wife, Moon, started shouting and climbed up into the sky above the roof. I waved and splashed and spouted for him to come back down, but he just hung there looking fierce. Things have been like that for centuries since. No, Ananse, I think it's better to leave Sun alone . . . '

'You needn't worry a drop more about it,' announced Ananse. 'Just one final thing, Water, before I go. You won't forget the drinks, will you?'

'Me, forget the drinks?' glugged and gurgled Water between his banks. 'Why, drinks are my business!'

So until their next meeting, Water flowed his way, Ananse scuttled his. No, not to the Sun which was far too far, but to the village post-office to send a special interplanetary invitation telex.

Ananse's party arrangements were now complete.

He stood outside his hut in his 'Been-To' hat and three-piece suit and Italian shoes, adjusted his Parisian bow-tie, consulted his Japanese watch, patted his local stomach and waited to welcome his guests. His insides tingled with excitement. So many opposites meeting in one place! What marvellous mayhem might follow! To make the time pass quicker, Ananse the Confusionist pictured to himself the evening's highlights in advance.

First there would be the spectacle of Stick attacking Fire with karate kicks and bony forearm smashes only to be reduced to ashes . . . Then there would be Fire fighting Water . . . Fire choking on his own steam . . . Water winning by a backward body-press, stranglehold, and half-Nelson . . . Then there would be the star fight of the evening: in the Cosmic Division, Water the Raining World and Current Oceanic Champion taking on the Mighty Sun himself, Interplanetary Belt Holder and Supreme Heavyweight and Lightweight Champion of the Universe . . .

And then, of course, the more the opposite guests struggled and fought and knocked and burned and drowned and radiated one another about, the less they would feel like sharing in the food they had promised to bring. The more food Ananse would have for himself. Yes, as Master and Disaster of Ceremonies he had it all worked out down to the last mouthful. Or so in his round stomach of stomachs he imagined. The fewer the merrier: that was Ananse's motto. At least it was when it came to eating . . .

Again Ananse consulted his watch. Again he adjusted his bow-tie. He was beginning to feel even hungrier than usual and from the way he tapped his Italian shoes, one to eight against the ground and back again, not a little irritated as well . . .

First arrivals were Farmer and Stick.

Farmer brought a sackful of yams from his farm and Stick brought many skewerfuls of freshly cooked meat, sliced onions and tomatoes tucked between.

The two guests wished their host many happy returns, first from his world tour, then for his birthday. And, of course, they did not forget to compliment him on his outfit.

Ananse, in turn, returned the returns and compliment with equally happy welcomes and thanks.

'Hmmmm, perhaps I should manage to have several birthdays a year, not one,' thought Ananse to himself as he helped Farmer and Stick unload their gifts. 'There is the Roman calendar, the Islamic calendar, the Ibo calendar, the Chinese calendar and the Ghana All-Star Musician calendar hanging in my bedroom. Why not then my own Spider's calendar, although in it every day would be a weekday and every other day a feast day, then birthdays whenever I chose.'

But he could work out the details later. It was time to make his first two guests feel at home. 'My house is your house,' announced Ananse and he proceeded to show them to the yard at the back of his hut where he had placed a row of chairs for the big occasion.

Then the sky, which had been blue before, turned a deep and stormy grey. Some drops of rain spotted the concrete floor. Who else was it but Water, carrying a cloud-sized calabash of fresh palm wine and enough beer and minerals to quench the thirst of a gaping volcano. He gushed and bubbled and fizzed all over the place and was quite the life and soul of the party until . . .

'What the blazes!' roared an angry all-too-familiar voice. 'I didn't expect to find you here!' Yes, Fire had just arrived in a cloud of smoke.

'And I didn't expect to find you!' spat Water in reply.

The two old and elemental enemies faced each other across the courtyard. Fire was about to add fuel to the fray when, startlingly, the sky cleared. The opposite guests were dazzled into silence. It was Sun, the special interplanetary guest of honour whom Ananse, in his capacity as First Spider in Outer Space, had first met during his famous rocket trip from the Cape Kennedy Space Centre. (But that is another tall tale for another time.)

'Sorry I am late,' blazed the giant red-faced newcomer. (It was almost sunset.) 'But I have had several thousand light years to travel.'

Then with Ananse's willing help, Sun began to unload his presents from the Skymobile parked brilliantly outside. The presents of the other guests paled in comparison. Where Farmer had brought along a sackful of yams, Sun had brought a whole harvest. Not just yams either, but every vegetable and fruit imaginable: dates, apples, pineapples, bananas, guavas, groundnuts, coconuts, watermelons, honeymelons, cherries, berries. But you can finish the list yourselves. Not that any of the guests were in the mood for food or merriment. Farmer felt the sweat sweltering alarmingly from his brow. Stick feared any moment he might burst into flames. Water was evaporating in buckets. Fire seemed the only guest not unduly put out by Sun's arrival.

Then, just to add confusion to confusion, along squiggled Snake, sporting a striped and brand-new skin. He was about to wish many happy returns and add his present to the rest when, quick as a hiss, he spotted Farmer. Here was his chance to settle old quarrels for good (or bad), the thought ran like poison from one end of his body to another.

'Help!' cried Farmer to Stick on seeing his old enemy poised for the attack. But the quarrelling had already become infectious. Stick was already engaged in a heated tussle with Fire. Shouting, hissing, beating, roaring, crackling, spitting, gurgling, blazing, flashing with earthly and unearthly heat, soon all the guests had started fighting. Opposite by opposite, Ananse's party was going wrong, just as the host had planned.

Taking a mighty helping of food and palm wine with

him, Ananse retired to the roof to enjoy the fruits and meat and vegetables of his confusion. Proudly and greedily he looked down on his mischief. Divide and rule. Let the guests' struggle and strife be his gain. And his food. And his drink. His guests could beat themselves to death for all he cared. He had got what he wanted. And their conflict was all the more pleasurable for being of his own making. Water was applying a half-Nelson on Fire who was biting the gnarled foot of Stick who was fending off a boa-constricting move by Snake who was hissing at Farmer who hardly knew whose side he was on any more . . .

Then Sun, more clear-headed than the other guests, had a flash of insight.

'Friends!' he boomed. 'So we are fighting one another when we should be making merry? Why? If we are to fight at all, we should be fighting the one who made us fight in the first place. And who is that but that cunning old confusionist Ananse? Yes, it is as clear as daylight. Remember the story of the sticks. One stick taken by itself can be broken easily. But once several sticks are joined together in one bundle, can they be broken so easily?'

'Not at all,' supported Stick who had now freed himself from the attentions of Fire and Snake.

'Well, so it should be with us. In unity is strength; in division confusion and weakness till even a tiny creature like Ananse can beat us. I ask you, is it not a big disgrace? Let us not then fight uselessly among ourselves, but let us unite and teach Ananse a lesson . . . '

But Ananse, on hearing Sun's booming voice, had vanished . . .

In the brilliant light of Sun's advice, the guests forgot their quarrels and were soon searching, searching for their host. Scattering cosmic rays and sparks, Sun cast his mighty headlamp eyes in all corners. Stick beat away the tangled grass. Snake buried his head curiously in beneath the ground. Then at last came a flashing shout from Sun. 'Here he is, everyone. You can stop looking.'

And there indeed Ananse was, deep inside the leaves of a mango tree.

'Come out of there, Ananse. Your party is over!' the guests proclaimed with one voice.

But Ananse is not Ananse for nothing. 'Leave me alone!' he shouted through his nose. 'So you think your peace means anything? No, you can't fool me. Water, you big cry-baby even at your age! Are you really going to let Sun bamdazzle you so easily? Can't you see he is evaporating you even now? Take hold of yourself and carry on fighting. And what about you, Sssssssnake, giving in to Farmer like that? Or do you want me to tell you all the wicked things Farmer says about you behind your back? And Stick, just because Fire is holding his breath and letting you alone, do you think he'll do the same next time? No condition is permanent. Ask Water, if you don't believe me . . . '

'Not so fast, Ananse. You are the enemy and not we ourselves,' countered the guests, their voice as one as ever.

And to prove their single-mindedness, Fire started sawing down the tree where Ananse was hiding. A creak, a crack, a leafy splash and shudder and the tree capsized, catapulting Ananse from inside it. Fast as his eight legs would carry him, Ananse scuttled into the bush.

But Water was keeping a beady eye on the trickster's movements. A running stream cut Ananse off in mid-flight. Poor puzzled and panting Ananse! He rolled his eyes three hundred and eighty degrees and back again. At zero to sixty degrees was Water, at sixty degrees was the cold-blooded Snake. At ninety-eight degrees were Farmer and Stick. At two hundred degrees or more was Fire, crackling and spitting. Directly overhead at three hundred and sixty degrees by the compass times as many degrees again by the thermometer hovered Sun, booming and flashing instructions.

Ananse was cornered and there was not a wriggle or a squiggle or jiggle he could do about it. Just to make sure, the six guests tied Ananse up with not one rope, but three, a different guest at each end and Ananse in the middle like a sort of hub.

'Let me go!' gasped Ananse. And again he started scuttling. But the more directions he scuttled the tighter the ropes squeezed him.

Yes. Ananse's party was over. Now nothing goes for nothing. Not only had he lost his round stomach. He was soon taken on a second world tour, a tour of shame. The tour was a great success and children of all nations turned up to see the famous trickster tricked by his own trick. Quite a few adults turned up too. The profits went to Sun and Peace Promotions International Ltd., the tour's organizers. And none of the guests quarrelled over who should receive what. The opposite guests had learned that unity is also good sense and they shared the money equally.

And what about Ananse? After his second tour and torture he was released and allowed to return to his village where he is now writing his Memoirs. Or so the bush telegraph goes.

Another report claims he has fled overseas in shame. Recently there have been sightings of Ananse as far away as Trinidad, Jamaica, and even Mexico. Whether he was there as a tourist or immigrant, the report does not say. Only that he was wearing sunglasses and disappeared before he could be asked any questions. Not that a trickish creature like Ananse would have had any difficulty in forging a passport or visa. Then on his two world tours he had made plenty of useful contacts. Brer Rabbit from America, Reynard the Fox from England, Touré the Hare from Senegal, Gizo (Ananse's distant cousin) from Northern Nigeria had all offered Ananse hospitality and shelter from the law or anything else. (The only inhospitable exception was Tortoise for reasons we will discover in our next story.) In fact, there is a rumour that Ananse is a leading candidate for Chairman and General Secretary of the next CIT (Community of International Tricksters) Annual Conference. Who knows? The bush telegraph puts out so many stories . . .

One thing is certain though. Ananse is not the same Ananse as before. Wherever he may be, sometimes he stares down at his waist where the three ropes had held him. Am I looking at myself or am I looking at a chewing stick? he wonders. Yes, his stomach, which was once round as a bowl of fufu, might have flown off like some UFO into outer space for all the chance he has of getting it back again. Under 'visible peculiarities' it is even written down in his passport: 'Apparent absence of belly.'

And that, kind listeners, is why spiders' waists are so thin, thin as the pen with which I have scribbled this story . . .

Ananse's Harvest

Anse the Spider and Tortie the Tortoise nowadays live apart. Tortie creeps and crawls his way. Ananse scuttles and sidewalks his, and never the two shall meet. No, not even in storybooks. Once, though, many harvests ago, the two small creatures were next door neighbours. Or next field neighbours, for they were both farmers and neither of their huts had anything as modern as a door.

Now things would have gone peacefully and storylessly along but for one big question neither creature could get out of his head. Ananse was clever, quite all right. Tortie was clever, quite all right. Everyone knew that, even to their cost. But which one was cleverer?

Neither could stomach the idea of his neighbour doing better or eating more than himself. Rivalry was never hotter than around harvest time. All year round it built up, then reached a green height of envy and suspicion. Tortoise would keep a beady eye on Ananse's farm. Ananse would keep an equally beady eye on Tortoise's farm. Potter envies potter, goes a proverb. Why not then, farmer envies farmer? Each of them wanted to know whose crop was biggest. It wasn't just greed. It was a matter of agricultural pride.

'Hmmmm! To take second place to a tortoise: what a big disgrace! I would sooner go on hunger strike!' Ananse announced to Anansia one mealtime, not knowing that in the next hut Tortie was just announcing to Tortesca: 'Hmmmm! To take second place to that sly and busybodyish spider when I have already beaten the hare! Never! I'll show him what farming is all about. And eating, if he is foolish enough to challenge me!'

When, then, Ananse sidewalked from the hole in his hut and saw Tortoise's crop towering above his own, he was not happy at all. Tortoise's field was so very green and tall that his own seemed a patch of weeds. Yet both farms shared the same type of soil. How in heaven or on earth did Tortoise manage it? At once Ananse suspected Tortie of all kinds (and unkinds) of trick. Perhaps Tortie had diverted the stream in his own direction. Ananse scuttled off to investigate. But the stream bubbled and twinkled innocently on as before, not a bank or bend out of place. Perhaps, then, Tortie was using some magic fertilizer. Or had he crept off to bribe the gods of rains to shower down their gifts unequally?

In fact, all the tricks Ananse wished he had used himself, he now blamed on his hump-shelled neighbour. Whatever the case, he must find out the secret of Tortie's success and stop it. And with immediate effect, for was not harvest time just round the corner?

Scuttling sideways, Ananse approached Tortie and said, 'But, Tortie, how in heaven or on earth do you do it? I mean, your crop looks so fresh and healthy I turn green just looking at it! As one next field neighbour to another, let me into your secret. I won't tell anyone, I cross my legs on it.'

'There's no secret,' retorted Tortie, putting down his hoe and wiping a bead of sweat from his bullet-shaped brow. 'No secret at all other than hard work. Yes, Ananse, honest straightforward hard work, that's all there is to it.'

A plain enough answer you might say. But not to Ananse. There was something in Tortie's voice he did not like. It was as if Tortie were laughing at him, and no, Ananse didn't like that at all. 'Hard work indeed! I'll give Tortie hard work!' Ananse replied to himself. 'And haven't I worked hard, too? Ask Anansia, aren't I up every sunrise and working until sunset? And yet my crop is not a patch on Tortie's.'

To prove how bad things were, Ananse began to lose his appetite.

Then, that night, he had a dream. Tortoise was celebrating the coming New Yam Festival. All his guests were assembled and enjoying well as well could be, while there was Ananse having to entertain them with eight-handed handstands and generally acting the fool. Worse still, he received only a few grains of rice for his pains. All the guests were cheering and Tortoise was laughing till his shell would break when, thank goodness, Ananse had woken up. No, and never may that dream come true, he vowed there on his bamboo bed. And as the insects sang away outside in the moonlight, Ananse thought out a plan. Yes . . . and yes . . . and yes . . . and yes . . . His mind span its web. All that remained was for Tortie to fall into it.

The sun rose, and there was Ananse sidewalking back to Tortie's field.

'Tortie, I have some very important news, straight from the Chief's own mouth,' announced Ananse.

'Well, what is it?' retorted Tortie, looking up from his yams.

'Chief says everybody must cut down his crop by tomorrow. No why's or but's about it. Anyone who refuses will be thrown into prison. I am only telling you this as a neighbour, you understand, and because I would hate to see you in trouble.'

And before Tortie could forward any awkward or plan-stopping questions, Ananse had vanished.

True to Ananse's lie, Tortie started digging up the yams he had spent all those months planting. It was bitter, but less bitter than being thrown into a slimy-walled, damp-floored dungeon. Tortie should know: he had spent two starving months there on a trickery charge some time before. Now the Chief had spoken, Tortie could only obey.

By midday Tortoise had dug up all his yams. Half-sized and every imaginable shape, they lay piled in front of him—some like prehistoric feet, others like underground torpedoes, some like overgrown knots of ginger, others unlike anything but themselves. Tortie's field, so tall and green before, was now a soily wreck. Having minded his own business, Tortoise put down his hoe, got back his breath, then turned his attention to his next field neighbour.

'Hey, Ananse,' he called over the cactus hedge. 'So aren't you going to start digging up your own crop as well? Remember the Chief's order. You would not want to spend the New Yam Festival in prison, would you?'

But Ananse was not listening. He was behind a tree drinking palm wine, while at his back his crop glistened peacefully in the sunlight. 'Hmm, victory is sweet,' announced Ananse to himself as he raised another calabash to his furry lips. 'Almost as sweet as this freshly-tapped palm wine!'

Slowly, surely, Tortoise realized what had happened. Chief's order, indeed! I will show Ananse Chief's order! But how? Now there was a question. Tortie buried his head in his shell. His mind shuffled plans like a computer, which one would work, which one would not. After a long while, Tortie's head came out with an answer. Hmm, if Ananse wanted a trial by trickery, he would have it. Any trick Ananse could do, Tortie could do better.

Slowly but surely enough, Tortoise was off on a one-man delegation to the Chief's own Palace to hear Ananse's story from the Chief's own mouth and . . . and . . . But we will come to that . . .

The Chief's Palace stood in the village centre, a mighty building of tall mud walls set one inside the other. Tortoise crept onwards and at last reached the Palace's innermost chamber. It was as cool and shadowy as outside was overbright and hot. There on a carved wooden stool sat the Chief in many-coloured robes.

'Welcome, Tortie, welcome,' proclaimed the Chief in a voice that was not at all unfriendly. 'Now, to what do I owe your visit?'

Adding a bit here, a bit there, for special effect, Tortoise told all.

' . . . To think of all that planting and cultivating, your Excellency, and now all wasted because of an order you never made! Of course, if I had known Ananse was deliberately playing tricks with your name, I would never have started digging . . . '

The Chief raised his hand to signify he had heard enough. 'So Ananse thinks he can play with my

Chieftancy, does he? Telling people to dig up their crops anyhow, why, that is economic sabotage! Or does he want my people to start starving? No, he needs to be taught a lesson.'

Tortoise nodded in agreement. Only there remained the question of how. Chief's dungeon was full already; then who knew what corrupting effect Ananse might have on the other prisoners? It was time for Tortie to whisper his plan in the Chief's ear. Nod, nod, nod went the Chief, and as he listened such a broad smile appeared it nearly knocked his gold-embroidered cap off.

'So you think my plan is a good one, your Excellency?' asked Tortoise.

'Excellent!' proclaimed the Chief.

His plan sealed with the Chief's smile of approval, Tortoise was off to put it into practice.

Back through the forest Tortoise crept and not so soon he reached the cactus hedge between his and Ananse's farm. He popped his head over and took a long look. Where was Ananse? He certainly was not working. Then Tortie heard the sound of groaning. There was Ananse sprawled beneath a mango tree. If he was not asleep he ought to have been. Two giant calabashes of palm wine balanced emptily to either side of him. His legs were tangled beneath his round body like a mixed-up eight times table and his eyes had a poached look. Too much palm wine had turned them murky yellow and flame-red at the edges. He blinked them into focus to see his all-too-familiar neighbour peering down at him. But what was that smile doing across his face?

'A happy harvest, Tortie?' Ananse heard himself saying through his headache.

'Yes. In fact, Ananse, I am so thankful to you . . . '

Thankful?!? Had Ananse's ears heard correct? This was not what Ananse had meant at all!

'Er . . . Thankful? Really? I don't quite understand . . . '

'Oh, yes,' continued Tortie, cheerful as can be. 'You see, I have just been to the Chief and he has promised me a special Farmer of the Year Award for harvesting my crop so early. I was rather surprised, I admit. My yams are small, I know, but the latest agricultural research has found crops should not be left in the ground too long . . . '

'Agricultural research?' Ananse repeated the strange expression.

'Yes. In fact, your advice has now been proven agronomically. You see, the best time for harvesting can be calculated by multiplying the carbohydrates by five, dividing by amino-acids, then taking the square root of the number of days since planting plus the sum of the Sun as it appears on the Moon's hypotenuse on day X, X here being equal to . . . '

Ananse's headache had begun to spread; his brain became a battleground of unknown quantities and figures. 'But what does all this mean?'

'Oh, it's quite simple when you think about it. It means that the sooner you dig up your crops, Ananse, the better.'

'But, Tortie, I told you exactly the same thing!'

'Just so. But that does not stop the advice being good, does it? Of course, I am only telling you as a neighbour . . . '

And with those words Tortie was gone. What was Ananse to do? Now Ananse could spot a trick as well as the next man. Or Tortoise. The truth, whatever it might be, could only be got from the Chief's own mouth. If Tortie was lying, then the truth would soon catch up with the creeping fellow. And Ananse would also be saved the useless labour of digging up his dearly-beloved yams before they were ready. Or so, despite his headache, Ananse reckoned.

If, on the other hand, Tortoise for some peculiar reason was really telling the truth, so be it. If not Farmer of the Year Award, Ananse might at least get the award for runner-up. Just as Tortoise had gained—however surprisingly—from Ananse's advice, so Ananse might gain from Tortoise's latest advice to him.

Hmmm. Hmmm . . . But headaches and too much thinking are not a good mixture. It was time to be up and walking. Ananse put his eight legs in order. Telling his wife to have a big bowl of pepper soup ready on his return, Ananse was on his way to the Chief's Palace and its cool and shadowy innermost chamber.

Next thing, Ananse had arrived. The Chief pulled his robes about his shoulders and looked down at the newcomer from his wooden stool, a mysterious smile upon his lips. Yes, Tortie's plan was working, and here was the spider in its web.

'Go on, Ananse, I am listening,' said Chief.

Ananse started to tell Chief what Tortoise had told him. Had Tortie really won 'Farmer of the Year Award'? And what about all that agricultural research or was it just a trickish smokescreen of Tortie's contorted imagination?

The Chief had heard enough. 'So you question the truth of my authority? You think I would side with liars?' he boomed and was about to call his guards when Ananse managed in the nick of time, 'Oh no, your Excellency, of course not . . . '

'Go, then, and dig up your crop just like Tortie dug up his,' decreed the Chief with immediate effect. 'Dawn tomorrow is the deadline. If any yams remain unharvested by then, the whole crop will be confiscated and declared village property.'

Ananse was in too much trouble to argue. He, too, knew the story of Tortie's ancestor who, hanging on with his teeth, had gone flying with the eagle, then, calling to the crowd below to watch, had foolishly opened his mouth . . . Ananse kept his mouth shut and was soon scuttling back to his farm. There was not a minute to lose. The sun was already setting. As Ananse calculated it, he had one full moon and a twelfth part of sun left till the Chief's deadline.

There was nothing else for it. Anansia and Ananse's four sons would have to be brought in to help. The sun went down; the moon came up. And there in its silvery light were Ananse and his family hoeing and digging yams.

'Need any help, Ananse?' enquired Tortoise, awakened by their groans of exhaustion.

Ananse could only say yes; though it made little difference, there was so little moon left. Then a cock crowed. Then the sun appeared, and along with it twelve of the Palace guards. The Chief had kept his word. No but's about it, the deadline had not been met and Ananse was forced to give up his crop.

Worse still, some weeks later under pain of hunger, Ananse was invited as compulsory guest to a banquet in honour of Tortie, 'Farmer of the Year'. And where did the food come from for this special and splendid occasion? From Ananse's farm, naturally. Ananse watched the yams and other vegetables he had spent all those months planting vanish in seconds down the throats of the assembled guests. And, of course, the Chief and Tortie between them made sure that nobody in the village had been left uninvited. There they all were eating and making merry. It was bitter, almost as bitter as having to listen to the congratulations and applause for his neighbour and rival. The Chief made a speech in Tortie's honour. Accompanied by the grasshopper on violin and the bullfrog on bass, the mynah bird sang a praise-song, and Tortie made another speech in reply. Then it was back to eating again. True, Ananse did not have to perform eight-handed handstands like in his nightmare. But that was small comfort when weighed against seeing his whole harvest being consumed before his eyes and all on account of Tortoise!

So Tortie had his hour of triumph and glory.

But it did not last. Back home again Tortie looked at Ananse's farm, then at his own. There was little or nothing to choose between them: two ruins, and only weeds to reap the difference. Ananse had tricked Tortoise. Tortoise had tricked Ananse. And now would Ananse try to trick Tortoise back? And would Tortie trickishly reply? No and never, the two animals agreed from the bottom of their empty stomachs. Yes, two tricksters is one too many, Ananse thought to himself. It was time for him to pack his things and move to another territory. One evening he called his wife and family. The next morning, six spidery shadows amidst shadows, the Ananse family were weaving their way westwards to set up farm where Ananse might carry on his tricks unrivalled.

And that is why Ananse scuttles and sidewalks his way, Tortie creeps and crawls his, and never the two shall meet. No, not in a hundred harvests. It suits them both just fine. In fact, absence seems to have made their hearts grow fonder. Each year, with the help of Monkey, Ananse sends the following telex over the bush telegraph: 'Lesson still not forgotten * Stop * Envy never enriched any man * Stop * Or spider * Stop * Yours Apologetically * Kweku Ananse.'

A meaningful rustling of leaves, and at the cost of a hundred groundnuts per word Tortie sends Monkey bounding off with the reply: 'Better to be envied than pitied * Stop * Best wishes for a long and happy stay in your new home and hopes for a better harvest * Stop * Tortie * Farmer of the Year * Stop.'

The Monster at the Stream

E lection fever was in the air. The jungle was there quite all right, but who was to be King of it? That was the question all the animals were assembled in a forest clearing to discuss.

The Lion anyway had no doubts about the matter. He sat on his hind legs, combed his mane with his claws, then cleared his throat.

'Grrrrrrrr!' A long roar ripped the air as if it had been a pocket handkerchief. Like it or not, the other animals were forced into silence.

'I am King of the Jungle. From Lagos to London, from Takoradi to Timbuctoo, every schoolchild knows that. Or if he doesn't, someone should teach him. All the story books agrrrrrree. So why waste our time making an election out of it?'

The animals did not agree.

But then they did not disagree either. They looked at those mighty molars, those incisive incisors, some fresh strands of meat caught between them. They looked at those claws clawing this way and that in emphasis. And they remembered the old story of how one day the lion,

81

the ass, and the dog had gone out hunting. Along the way the three animals had come across a dead goat. All three of them were hungry, but who was to get all that meat? After some discussion the three animals decided to share the meat equally between them. The goat's carcass was divided into three. No sooner had the ass stepped forward to take his share as agreed than the lion jumped on him. After devouring the ass's share of the dead goat, Lion devoured the poor living ass as well. According to the agreement the dog had every right to protest. However, on seeing what had happened to the ass and the lion spitting out his bones, the dog only prostrated himself and said in as pleasing a voice as he could muster, 'O your Lordship, take my share as well. In fact it would be an honour if you accepted.' The lion smiled at the dog's invitation. And so the dog, who had just come within a whisker of being eaten, saved his skin and all his bones as well.

No, it did not pay to meddle with a lion . . .

So now that the lion repeated his claim, 'I am King of the Jungle, or does anyone disagrrrree?', now that he bared his teeth once more, the other animals kept silent. They remembered what had happened to the ass all those years ago. However, even a tyrant likes to be liked by his own subjects, at least at the beginning. So after proclaiming himself king by a unanimous vote, the lion proclaimed the next evening a great feast to honour his new and prestigious appointment. It would be a matter of compulsory enjoyment for all. King Lion commanded the pleasure of the animals' company. No excuses for absence would be accepted.

Next morning came and with it preparations for the feast. The food was there quite all right, as was an artillery of pestles and mortars for pounding fufu. There only remained the problem of water for the cooking itself. Mrs Antelope—Antelopia by name—a tall, graceful lady with a long nose and golden skin and wide staring eyes, volunteered to go with a bucket to the nearby stream.

An easy and ordinary enough task, you might say, especially for a fast runner like Mrs Antelope. But when Mrs Antelope returned, she was in such a state that it was obvious something very extraordinary had happened. Mrs Antelope's long legs trembled beneath her and it was soon noticed that her bucket was missing.

'But what happened?' enquired Tortesca, the wife of Mr Tortoise. 'You look like you just saw a ghost.'

'It's . . . it's . . . it's . . . ' Before Mrs Antelope could say more, her wide staring eyes rolled shut and she had fainted with shock just at the memory of whatever it was she was trying to relate.

'This is serious,' agreed the wives of various species who had gathered to cook. 'And what's more, how can we prepare yams for the feast without water?'

It was decided to send Mrs Hippopotamus—Hippopotama to her friends—down to the stream instead. 'Hmmmm, now there goes a tough no-nonsense madam if ever there was one,' squeaked Mrs Mouse, the sound of Hippopotama's footsteps booming in her tiny ears. 'And as for thick skins, hers is the thickest. Whatever it is beside the stream that has so scared Pia will not scare our Hippopotama, that is for sure.'

Or not so sure.

Within half-an-hour Hippopotama was back, minus bucket and shaking so terribly that the whole forest shook with her in a dance of fear.

'It's . . . it's . . . it's . . . '

Again Hippopotama's explanation was evidently too terrible for words and, thickest skin or no, she could say no more. It was useless to chide with 'Pull yourself together!' or 'Are you a hippopotamus or a mouse?' since in a moment she too fainted like Antelopia.

It was time to bring in the men.

Mr Antelope bravely and nobly agreed to follow in his wife's footsteps down to the stream. And if it was not customary for men to carry water, then the occasion was a special one. If there was to be a feast, there must be water. And so, hanging a bucket from one of his horns, Mr Antelope set out.

And came back, a very different Mr Antelope from before. What had been a terror to the females was also a terror to the males. Again no bucket. Again no water. Again fear setting a seal on things, stamping out all explanation. Who was brave—or foolish—enough to go next? That was the question all the animals were now asking, each hoping the answer would not fall upon himself. Mr Hippopotamus was approached.

'Err . . . errrr,' he began, clearing the bullfrog from his throat and shifting from one fat foot to another. 'Errr, you see, I'm afraid my wife is still not herself. Nervous breakdown and hypertension, you know . . . I have to look after her. Terrible nightmares she has, even during daytime. No, as her one and only husband, I'm afraid I can't leave her on her own, however I might wish to. I hope you'll excuse me . . . '

The hyena was approached. 'Me?! Me, Hyena, go to the stream? You must be joking!' he laughed, baring his yellow teeth.

The leopard and the cheetah were approached. The

kangaroo invited for the feast all the way from Australia
was approached. The polar bear invited down from the
Arctic circle was approached. The armadillo and the
anteater were approached, as were the bushrat and
bristling porcupine, the upside-down bat, and the all-
ways-up baboon. Fear of whatever it was by the stream
had gripped them all by the feet and tails. Though none of
them said it directly, they were all too scared. Excuses of
all different twists and turns were produced. The polar
bear complained of heatstroke. The lizard and the snake
were allergic to water. The upside-down bat had
something wrong with his radar and could not find the
spare parts to fix it. The anteater, truthfully enough, said
he had no hands, how then could he carry a bucket, while
the all-ways-up baboon vanished into some secret corner
of the trees before anybody could embarrass or question
him further. As for the mice and insects, they thanked
God for making them so small nobody thought it worth
approaching them in the first place.

What the females could not do, it seemed the males
could not—or would not—do either.

There was only one animal left. Who else but Lion
himself? After all, was he not King and by his own
proclamation? And was not the great feast in his honour?
Out of pride he had no choice but to accept the challenge.
Besides, Lion was hungry, very hungry. Mrs Lion—
Leonora to her friends—gave her husband a bucket and a
heartening kiss on the whiskers. And so Lion left, plus
bucket, for the stream and whatever terrible or not-so-
terrible thing it was that dwelt there. No, he was not
afraid. Not yet, anyway.

'Grrrr,' he growled and grumbled through the
undergrowth. 'These my subjects are such cowards. They

should just count themselves lucky to have a king like me to protect them.'

No sooner had the lion reached the streamside, no sooner was he about to lower the bucket towards the twinkling water than, like a ghost with toothache, came a voice from deep, deep within the shadow:

'WHO GOESSS THERE? LET ME GREET HIM.
WHO GOESSS THERE? LET ME MEET HIM.
WHO GOESSS THERE? LET ME EAT HIM.'

The hairs on the lion's mane began to bristle like a bush in Harmattan. His teeth began to chatter like a train going over a level crossing, not in anger, not in hunger, but in fear. If this voice was so terrible, what might the voice's face, the voice's teeth, the voice's claws, the voice's stomach be like? Terribler than terrible. And before he got to witness them, King of the Jungle or no, Lion had turned three hundred and sixty degrees on his tail. Feast or no feast, water shortage or no water shortage, fufu or no fufu, Lion was running towards the safety of the village as fast as his legs would carry him. And as for the dent to his reputation, what use was reputation if you were not alive to enjoy it? Lion did not dare look back and only prayed that whatever-it-was by the stream did not have jaguar legs as well.

By the time Lion reached the door of his hut he was panting and trembling like he would never stop. 'Leonora, my queen, let . . . let . . . let . . . let me . . . in . . . I beg!'

Leonora was not pleased to see this trembling shadow of her husband at all. 'So this is what you have appointed yourself king for? So this was why I kissed you on the whiskers? King indeed! It's a disgrace. And as for me being your queen, I can hear the tongues of the neighbours wagging already. So you expect me to go out, and meet their laughter? If you don't take care, my husband, I will go and marry elsewhere, to a real lion and not a liar and a coward. Look at you. Are you a lion or a mouse? That is what I want to know,' she growled, before Lion had time to even get his breath back. 'And all because of what? Because of just a single bucket of water.'

Tortoise, speaking for the other animals, put the case a bit more politically.

'Friends, animals, countrymen, lend me your ears. I have a proposal to make. We see Lion here—our king self-proclaimed and self-appointed—shaking like a mango leaf in a thundershower. From a lesser and humbler animal we might expect such behaviour, but from a lion, never. Is this what we want in a leader? Is this what we look up to in a king? No, my fellow animals, it is not. I propose that we find a replacement with immediate effect.'

All the animals nodded in agreement. But who would the replacement be? Tortoise had foreseen the question and had a nice and rounded answer on the tip of his tongue.

'I . . . I, Tortoise, will go to the stream to fetch water. Just fetch me a bucket and it is as good as done. If I return with water inside, small and humble as I am, I ask to be made King. Or if not King, President so I can proclaim a special Presidential dinner in honour of my appointment.' Tortoise paused here and ducked his head inside his shell for a quick look at his notes which he had written out a short time before. 'If . . . If, though, I come back without bucket or without water, trembling like Lion here is trembling, then curse me for a loudmouth and a boaster, a useless somebody. In public I will eat my words with the strongest and most punishing alligator pepper in Mrs Alligator's kitchen.'

All the animals cheered Tortoise's daring proposal (all except Lion, that is) although they were very doubtful as to its success. How could a tiny creature like Tortoise succeed where a fierce and mighty creature like Lion had failed? It might be possible in storybooks, but the real life of the jungle was something different. All this, not to mention the problem Tortoise would have when it came to running away. Still, Tortoise was Tortoise—always had a surprise trick or two up his shell, volumes of them in fact. Who knew what Tortoise might think up this time?

'Your bucket, please, my sweet?' Tortoise gallantly appealed to Tortesca in the crowd. 'I am here to serve not be served . . .'

Despite Tortesca's protests that she was too young to be made a widow, eventually the bucket was brought. Off Tortoise went to face the whatever-it-was that awaited him by the stream.

'A brave little fellow,' commented Owl from the safe lookout of his perch as Tortoise dwindled from view. 'But foolish, most foolish. That thing by the stream will chop him like groundnut and probably not even bother to spit out the casing.'

Nevertheless, Tortoise was on his way and there was no stopping him, 'Slow But Steady' printed in invisible paint across his shell. At longer than long last he reached the stream. Noon had come and gone, and the place was thronging with long shadows.

Slowly Tortoise lowered his bucket into the water. No

sooner did it touch the surface than again came the voice, like a ghost with toothache:

'WHO GOESSS THERE? LET ME MEET HIM.
WHO GOESSS THERE? LET ME GREET HIM.
WHO GOESSS THERE? LET ME EAT HIM.'

Unlike Lion, Tortoise did not run. Or walk. Or creep. Or crawl. He calmly stood his ground and waited for the last echo of the voice to subside back into the greenish dark. Then, in a voice just as terrible, one word weaving eerily into the next, Tortoise replied:

'WHO GOESSS THERE? LET ME MATCH
    HIM.
WHO GOESSS THERE? LET ME CATCH
    HIM.
WHO GOESSS THERE? LET ME SCRRRATCH
    HIM.'

There followed a nerve-racking silence. Five seconds, ten seconds, half a minute, the dark green water lapping ominously in the half-light. Who was the owner of the terrible voice? What revenge would he-she-or-it take for Tortoise's impertinent and rash reply. Where would the he-she-or-it come out or up or down or round from?

The whole jungle waited . . .

Then . . . then there came a faint rustling from the far bank, a shimmering of leaves. Then there appeared in the shadows no monster, no ghost, no foul fiend, no bogeyman or bloody-bones or headcrusher, no being from outer space, no amazing hulk or giant or ten-headed ogre or television-handed ghostess but simply . . . a crab scarcely larger than your thumbnail, dragging behind him a stereophonic cowhorn trumpet with automatic built-in speakers. So that was the owner and terrible transmitter of the mystery voice? That was the terror of the jungle?

Tortoise held his sides in laughter.

Crab held his sides in laughter and did a hilarious and circular shuffle up the bank.

The forest echoed long and loud with their 'Ho's' and 'Ha's' so that even the animals back in the village could hear them. For the life of them they tried to guess what was happening. Had the monster at the stream gone mad? Had he swallowed Tortoise and Tortoise got stuck in his throat? Thinking over the dreadful possibilities, the animals were not amused at all. Their imaginations ran wild conjuring the ghastly fate that awaited them.

Imagine, then, their surprise when there at the entrance to the village appeared their very own Tortoise carrying a bucketful of water, Crab shuffling tinily behind.

So Tortoise had succeeded where all the other animals had failed. By popular vote Tortoise became first President Elect of the Jungle. For the rest of the evening the forest resounded merrily with the drumming of pestle against mortar, the fanfare of the promised Presidential feast. Soon the food was ready, delicious mountains of fufu rising from orange seas of palmnut soup, the main pounding having been done by Mrs Elephant, moving the gluey yam and plantain with her trunk between blows of the pestle.

'To Tortoise, our President and Liberator!'

'To Tortoise, our President and Liberator!' the toast echoed into the trees. And the animals raised full calabashes of palm wine in Tortoise's honour, Antelopia a glass of precious water.

You can be sure they had recovered from their excuses. Hippopotama had got over her nervous breakdown and hypertension so well that she danced a highlife with her husband. This time all the forest shook, not in fear, but in historical celebration, the baobab tapping its roots along with the rhythm. And if the snake and the lizard had been allergic to water, they were not at all allergic to palm wine judging by the calabashes they emptied. The all-ways-up baboon, who had reappeared sometime during the cooking, did a breakdance that had even Leonora laughing. As for the bat's broken-down radar, some spare parts must suddenly have arrived from somewhere, for the creature was now dancing upside-down without touching the ground.

And what about Lion? What else was there to do but wish himself an ostrich (or perhaps a crab) and bury his head in the sand? The other animals' celebration was his disgrace and he kept to the gloom of his hut. Hearing Leonora laugh he felt gloomier still. 'Grrrr,' he growled. 'If only I could get hold of Tortoise's secret weapon.' For how else could he have succeeded on his mission?

Of course Lion did not know there had never been a secret weapon. And of course Tortoise never told anybody, not even his wife, that the monster was only a crab scarcely bigger than your thumbnail. In the middle of the dancing Tortoise called Crab quietly aside behind a tree-trunk and made him sign an oath of secrecy to that effect. 'After all,' whispered President Tortoise into Crab's ear— wherever a crab's ear might be—'one good mystery deserves another.'

'Quite so, Tortie, quite so,' replied Crab in a voice that had shrunk back into normal size or smaller.

And so with a flourish of Crab's claw the agreement of secrecy was signed and secretly deposited in a specially-dug hole along with the stereophonic cowhorn trumpet and the built-in double speakers.

And who by a subsection of the same document became Tortoise's Vice-President, Campaign Organizer, Chief Political Adviser, and Minister of Information, Bush Telegraphs, and Telecommunications?

Crab, naturally. Which all goes to show that a couple of ounces of cunning can outweigh several tons of muscle. And that, kind listeners, is the history of how Tortoise became President of the Jungle and how King Lion was overthrown.

The Trap of Thanklessness

I t has been called a monster, albeit an invisible one. It has been called a serpent's tooth. It has been called a marble-hearted fiend. It has been called a door slammed shut in the face of kindness. What is it?

The answer is ingratitude, so easy to commit, so difficult to bear. Ingratitude. Caused not so much by what we do as by what we fail to do. The tall tale retold we are about to hear shows ingratitude in action. We meet one ungrateful person caught by his own ingratitude. Or one ungrateful animal. Once again we are back in the magical timeless world of ancestral folk tales where tortoises and lions and warthogs talk (not to mention talking skulls), where horses and carpets can fly, where a spider can beat an elephant, and where a mosquito can fall in love with an ear—and out of love again! But that is another tale for another time. Let us get back to our story . . .

The forest grunted.

Papa Warthog and his family were returning from planting groundnuts and were having a conversation along the way. The conversation was in their own language, of course, so let me translate, grunt by grunt . . .

'Now, my children, the jungle is a dangerous place, so keep to the paths and do not go nosing around where you don't know what might happen to your nose or anything else,' Papa Warthog was warning his children in Gruntish.

'Yes, Papa,' agreed the small warthogs, and they fell into single file behind their father, Mama Warthog bringing up the rear. Then, as if in echo of Papa Warthog's words, a roar tore the air. Again the roar came, and then again, like an aeroplane crashing through the sound barrier and leaving behind it an awkward and threatening silence. What could it be? However much it sounded like one, it could not be a plane because planes were yet to be invented; the only man to fly at that time was not a man, but Tortoise. But then that is another story for another place and time . . .

The warthogs kept nervously walking, their noses to the ground. Then, round the next bend in the pathway, they saw the owner of the terrible roars. It was a lion. Not an ordinary lion but a lion hanging upside down in mid-air. And how had the lion got into such an awkward position?

He had got caught in a hunter's trap, one of those consisting of a rope tied tightly between the branch of a tree at one end and a peg in the ground at the other end, a sort of giant fishing rod to catch not fish but bushrats, antelopes, warthogs . . . and sometimes lions. The lion had been strolling proudly along one evening and had unknowingly put his paw in the loop of rope on the ground. Then whoooosh! Bedoynnng! He had been lifted into the air as easily as a crate of cargo is lifted by a dockside crane.

Not only that. For three long days Lion had had nothing to eat but the occasional fly or misguided mosquito. His paws ached like a toothache in the wrong place. His mane hung downward like a giant beard.

Seeing Lion dangling there, the Warthogs held a family conference. Should they rescue Lion or should they just leave him hanging in mid-air? To help a fellow animal in trouble was all to the good. A hundred proverbs said so. But what if the animal was a lion and the animal was hungry like Lion was hungry? Might not the lion reward the Warthogs' kindness by eating them dead or alive? One was as bad as the other. Eventually, however, kindness won out against all odds. The Warthogs decided to take the risk and set Lion free. Papa Warthog approached the lion and started to untie him.

'Oh, thank you, thank you, thank you,' growled Lion in Lionish.

But the way Lion was looking at Papa Warthog's children, it definitely seemed the lion's thank you's came from his stomach rather than from his heart.

'This lion, I don't trust him at all. His whole face spells danger,' grunted Baby Warthog in Gruntish.

Papa Warthog decided the same thing. But he did not say it. Old age and the cruel law of the jungle had taught him the value of keeping quiet at crucial moments.

'Papa Warthog, one good turn deserves another. I hope you and your family have time to accompany me to my den so I can return your kindness. But I am so hungry and . . . and . . . ' Lion checked himself. But his bloodshot eyes and his teeth aimed at Baby Warthog's body said as much as any words. The cat was out of the bag. Or the lion, rather!

'Oh, Mister Lion, that's very kind of you,' grunted Papa

Warthog in Lionish. 'But we are in a hurry. Another time perhaps. Hoggatha, my dear, are the children all here? Good. Well, Mister Lion, we have to be off but, er, just allow me to ask you one small question?'

'Go ahead,' said Lion, shaking his paws to get the circulation flowing again.

'Well, Mister Lion, we were wondering, my family and I, how . . . err . . . exactly did you manage to get yourself in such a strange trap in the first place?'

'It was like this, you see,' replied Lion. 'First I put my foot in the rope like this . . . '

All eyes and ears, Papa Warthog assisted Lion to retie the rope to the peg and so carry on his demonstration.

'Good, yes, just like that, you've got it,' said Lion, enjoying his role as teacher.

'And then what happened?' asked Papa Warthog like the ideal pupil.

'As I was saying, I put my foot in the loop of rope . . . '

'How exactly?'

'At speed and without looking where I was going.'

'Would you demonstrate?'

'Of course, Papa Warthog, seeing you are so interested.' And the lion took a run. His front paw got caught in the loop of rope. Whooosh! Bedoyyyng! Next moment he was hanging in mid-air just like when the Warthogs had met him.

'So that is what really happened?' enquired Papa Warthog, pretending to be very impressed.

'Yes, exactly,' said Lion. 'It was quite a surprise, I can tell you.'

'And very painful, I should think?'

'Very painful!' assured Lion from mid-air, his legs thrashing about like a drowning swimmer's.

'Hmmm, and what happened then, I wonder?'

'Well, you see, I was suffering more and more, and then you came and rescued me.'

'And then what happened?'

'Then . . . er . . . er . . .'

But whether through guilt or something else Lion had suddenly stopped.

'Yes, Lion, don't lie. You wanted to eat my children, didn't you? That's what happened. So is that how one good turn deserves another? I wish you goodbye, Mister Lion. Or should I say badbye.'

'But you can't leave me hanging in mid-air like this. Who will rescue me again? Papa Warthog, come back, I beg, come back—oh . . .'

But Papa Warthog had already vanished down the path. Again a terrible roar tore the air. But this time Papa Warthog and his family did not bother to find out where it came from. They just kept their noses to the path and went on walking in single file, Mama Warthog bringing up the rear. They had learned their lesson. Ah, inGRPRRRRatitude! Lion's roaring tore the air once more. Yes, ingratitude was painful.

'That Mister Lion, don't mind him,' finalized Mama Warthog in Gruntish.

And so the warthogs got home safely.

And so Lion was left hanging in the trap of his own thanklessness.

Or at least he was left hanging until one day, several days later, a bushrat happened to enter the story.

There was Lion upside-down, a skeleton of his former self, his paws aching like a toothache in the wrong place, nothing to eat but a misguided fly or mosquito who fell in and out of love with ear, though that is another story.

97

Bushrat, whose nose till then had been buried in the grass, looked up and was about to run away and out of the tale completely. (He feared the tale might have a terrible ending.) But this time Lion did not bite or snap or rip or roar or claw or open his jaws to swallow him or try to tear the atmosphere into invisible pieces. He did not even growl. In fact, Lion could not have been fierce even if he had wanted. He just asked in a voice as polite as polite could be: 'Bushrat, my grass-cutting friend, I hope it wouldn't be asking too much for you to stop your grass-cutting a moment and kindly do me a favour. You won't regret it, I swear.'

'Well, er, if you say so, Lion,' replied Bushrat in Lionish which also happened to be the jungle's official language.

'It's these ropes, you see. I don't know how I can undo them and, oh, I am so tired of hanging here in mid-air . . . '

Bushrat took a long look at the mechanics and aerodynamics of the situation. Then he saw the answer. He climbed up on to the lion's body and using the lion's stomach as a platform, he positioned himself beside one of the ropes. Next, he was putting his grass-cutting skills to a new purpose. His two front teeth cut slowly but surely through the fibre. The taste was not as good as grass, but it was all in the cause of friendship. One rope was gnawed through; one of Lion's legs went free. Two ropes were gnawed through; two of Lion's legs went free. Six ropes were gnawed through; Lion's body was now free completely. The tree twanged upright and Lion did a backward flying, high-powered somersault on to the grass below. He was now soundly on his own four feet just like before. Or almost . . .

No, he did not eat Bushrat for his dinner, as you might be fearing. Nor did he look at him hungrily as he had looked at Baby Warthog. What with all that hanging in mid-air, his claws aching like toothache in the wrong place, nothing to eat but a misguided fly or mosquito who fell in and out of love with ear, but that is another story, Lion had had plenty of time to ponder on what had happened with the warthogs. He had learned his lesson, InGRRRRRatitude did not pay.

'Thank you, thank you, thank you,' he addressed Bushrat, hardly a growl in his voice. Though this time he really meant it. 'And any time you need help, just call me on the bush telegraph. No problem. No act of kindness is ever wasted.'

Many times since that once upon a time, Lion has saved Bushrat from ending up in the cooking pot, just like Bushrat saved Lion from the trap of thanklessness. If, then, bushrats are a scarce commodity in Eating Rooms nowadays, do not blame Austerity or the state of the economy or the destruction of the rainforest, the bushrat's natural and age-old habitat. Blame it on Lion's kindness. Lion, in return for Bushrat's favour, has adopted the bushrat as his protected species. Bushrat is thankful. Lion is thankful. And that, kind listeners, is the end of the story, the tail of the tale, and, for that matter, of our tales also, a farewell full stop.

Afterstory, also by Moonlight

Back under that mango tree, large and gnarled and leafy as wildest wish can measure, it is nearly midnight. Storiouser and storiouser, one tall tale has led to another with the audience not at all unwilling to join in with a tale of their own or make somebody else's tale taller still.

Already that moon has sailed half-way across the sky. To see even shadows by, once more comes its hush, plus, if you listen closer, the punctuation of a distant bullfrog.

Yes, it's time to call it a night.

Story-teller's drum notwithstanding, some of the younger listeners fell asleep several stories ago. Leaving our tricksters to their own devices, our story-teller puts away his array of gestures and voices, then shrinks quietly back into his actual self.

One of the older listeners yawns.

A cloud shaped not unlike Kweku Ananse himself flits across the moon's spotlight.

A firefly flickers by.

In a few hours the sun will come up. Our story-teller

has a tale about that also. Only he is tired as well and tomorrow is another day . . .

Other books in the series

Tales from Africa
Kathleen Arnott
ISBN9780192750792

Meet a greedy spider, an evil shark, flying horses, and a cunning hare. You'll find all these and more in these exciting tales from Africa. You'll also find the answers to questions like why flies buzz and why the sun and moon live in the sky.

Tales from the West Indies
Philip Sherlock
ISBN9780192750778

Inside the pages of this book you'll meet a variety of unforgettable characters, including the wily monkey, unlucky Mr Snake, and, of course, cunning Anansi the spider and his old adversary, Tiger.

This lively collection of tales brings to life the rich tradition of storytelling in the West Indies and Guyana.